Contents

Cover art by Lex Villena

© Ben Sixsmith 2021

Hero

Martin stood behind the till and looked around the shop with the cold, measured gaze of a security guard. The big man's lime green polo shirt made him look as if he had stolen a school uniform. It clung to him for its life.

Across the shop, a young man and woman were looking at a washing machine. Martin warmed, remembering when he and Emma had equipped their first flat. He strolled across, beaming what he hoped was a benign smile.

"Can I help?"

The couple turned around with a start. They froze, as if confronted by an angry bull, before realising that he was an employee. The young man, in a leather jacket and a beanie, relaxed and smiled.

"We're just looking, thanks."

"Do you have any other colours?" asked the woman, trailing her fingers unimpressedly across one model.

"Erm, no."

The couple made their excuses and left. Martin wondered if he could have said anything more. *No, but we can order one. No, but there's some paint in the back. No, but have you considered that it's a fucking washing machine.* He looked at his phone. 10.37. It felt like it had been 10.37 for an hour. At least when people had used analogue clocks you could see *some* progress.

2

"Martin, have you got a minute?"

It was Paul, the manager. He looked even more unsmiling than usual. His thin, Bela Lugosi face looked tired and drawn. He walked like the cucumber Martin had always assumed was lodged inside his rectum had been driven an inch deeper.

"Sure."

He followed Paul into his office - a cramped and cluttered room that seemed more like a broom cupboard. A woman was standing there. She had the lean body of a marathon runner and a short, orange hairdo that was simultaneously austere and childish. She looked Martin up and down like a farmer inspecting livestock.

"This is Sandra from Human Resources," said Paul.

"Pleased to meet you," said Martin.

"Likewise," she said, sounding even less pleased to meet him than he was to meet her.

"We wanted to have a little chat with you, Martin," said Paul, trying to push his sleeves without unbuttoning his cuffs.

"A chat?"

Martin did not think he meant the kind with tea and biscuits.

"We've had a report that you used inappropriate language," said Sandra.

"Eh?"

"You were talking to a customer and you referenced an "Islamicist prick"."

The words rang a bell, and he half-remembered the conversation. He saw no point in denying it.

"I'm sorry for swearing."

"It isn't about the swearing," said Sandra, ""Islamicist"? You don't think that is offensive to Muslims?"

"What? No, I don't mean Muslims! I mean the, er – I mean the Muslims who want to make everybody *else* Muslims."

"Isn't that "Islamist"?" Paul asked.

"What? Oh. Maybe."

"*Regardless*," said Sandra, folding her arms, "How do you think a Muslim customer or colleague would have felt if they had heard such language?"

"Adil is my only Muslim colleague and he's in Ibiza," Martin blustered, "The only people there were me and this bloke who recognised me from back in the day. Oh, and Tim. It was Tim who told you wasn't it? I *thought* I saw him snooping. He's always been holier than thou."

"It doesn't matter who was there," said Sandra, stubbornly, "It matters what was said."

"Just to be clear, I was telling a story about how I stopped a terrorist."

"I kno---"

"About *how I stopped a terrorist.*"

"We appreciate that Martin," Paul said, trying gallantly to lower the temperature, "We're not being anti-Martin here."

"Of course not," said Sandra.

"We're not trying to punish you or make you feel bad. We just think that in this day and age, you – all of us – could use some extra training."

"Training?"

"Sensitivity training," said Sandra.

"Look, I sell washing machines," protested Martin, "If you want me to be carefuler, that's fine, but I don't need any of *that* bollocks."

Sandra's lips retreated in on themselves but it was Paul who looked angriest. He had not kicked, and scratched, and clawed his way into becoming boss of a home appliance shop to have to deal with such blatant insubordination. He bunched his fists.

"Bollocks? Bollocks is it?"

"You know what I---"

"If you're going to ignore simple instructions then I don't need any of *your* bollocks."

"Paul, I just mea---"

"Do you know what could happen to this shop if someone heard you talk like that? I'm not going to take that risk. No. I'm sorry, but we're going to have to let you go."

Martin stood and left the room without saying a word. He walked out of the shop, picking up his jacket as he went, and headed for the tube. As he strode through the grey London morning, he saw a gaggle of protesters waving Palestinian flags. *"Takbir!"* *"Allahu Akbar!"* Perfect.

On the tube, Martin sat back and closed his eyes. Then he opened them.

He remembered that morning like no other. It was only natural. He had talked about it countless times. He had been on the tube, coming home from a long night at work, listening to Iron Maiden on his walkman. Around him were tired workers, travelling to and from their shifts, excitable holiday makers, clutching their suitcases, and exhaustingly drunk clubbers sleeping through their stops. Opposite him was a young man who looked Indian or Pakistani. He had his hood up and was fiddling with his shoes. Martin looked at him. What the hell was he doing?

That was when he saw the little flame of a lighter. Martin burst to his feet, leapt across the train and smacked his knee, with all the force that he could summon, into the young man's face. He heard the satisfying crunch of broken bone.

The man dropped to his knees, but was still fumbling with his shoes. Martin fell across him and landed on his back. He thrust his arm around his neck and flung himself backwards, hearing a choking sound as he tightened his grip.

Martin felt pain explode behind his ear. Someone had kicked him in the head.

"Get off him bruv!"

"He's got a bomb," Martin snarled.

The man behind him saw the smoking shoes.

"Oh, shit! Call the police!"

"We're on the *underground*," barked Martin, as he felt the terrorist go limp and loosened his hold a little, "Sit on his fucking legs."

For a while, everything was great. He was in all the papers. He appeared on *This Morning*. He met the Prime Minister, who shook his hand and said something about how he represented "the best of the British spirit." He received a Queen's Gallantry Medal - though, sadly, from Prince Charles rather than Her Maj. His local promised him free drinks for life.

But then it all went away. People stopped calling. People stopped recognising him. Emma got sick. He started drinking heavily. Emma got *more* sick. He drank *more* heavily. Emma died. He sobered up, for their daughter's sake, but he had to stop working as a doorman because being around alcohol was too much to handle. That was how he got into retail. Now he had lost even that.

"What do you mean you lost your job?" asked Amanda on the phone, "How did you lose *that* job?"

"I don't know," shrugged Martin, "Political correctness. You can't say anything these days."

He scooped a pile of tomato-splattered cardboard into the bin. He always noticed how messy his flat was when he talked to Amanda. He knew he should take more care of it. He and Emma had just finished paying off the mortgage when she had been taken ill.

"Why were you talking about *anything* except washing machines?"

"Someone recognised me," sniffed Martin, "That doesn't happen every day you know."

"What are you going to do now?"

"Find a better job."

It sounded simple. How hard could it be? It was not as if he was looking for six figures, bonuses and a company car. Well, it turned out to be difficult. Very difficult. He should have guessed. He was a 50-year-old man with a dodgy back who had only ever worked as a doorman and a shop assistant.

"Do you have any qualifications?" asked the manager of a coffee shop, eyeing the "education" section of his CV, which began and ended with his secondary school.

"I have a Queen's Gallantry Medal."

"No shit. Why?"

"Choking out a terrorist."

Martin wasn't sure that the man believed him, but either way he can't have thought it qualified him to serve cappuccinos as he never rang back.

Anger stewed inside him. What kind of treatment was this? Okay, he knew it could have been anyone on that train. If he had stopped to take a piss it might have been someone else. But it *hadn't* been someone else, it had been *him*, and after a few months of being treated like a hero he had been forgotten. Now he turned on the TV and found that people were being celebrated for scoring goals and deciding that they wanted to be called "they" rather than "he". Was that fair?

He didn't have anyone to complain to. He had lost a lot of friends when he had stopped drinking, and a lot of friends immediately before he had stopped, and he did not want to burden the few that he had kept with his complaints.

Then he remembered Twitter. He had opened an account around ten years before, and had enjoyed a flurry of attention before realising that he had nothing to say. It was the perfect platform. Somehow, he remembered his password: "12345678".

"Lost my job because I didnt want "sensitivity training"," he posted, "Cant get another. Nice way to treat a man after 30 years of honest work. Oh and kicking a terrorist in the face."

He got some nice responses. "Sorry to hear that pal." "This fucking country." "Call yourself a woman. Then they'll call you a hero again." Some were not so nice. "Sounds kind of racist." "Shut up, gammon." "Nice knee. Shame about the brain."

Martin thought that that was that until he got a direct message from Henry Sutcliffe. Henry Sutcliffe, a Twitter bio informed him, was, "Columnist @Telegraph, wine critic @TheSundayTimes, author of "The Death of Reason" and "The Feminist Delusion""." "Hello," the message said, "Sorry for sending this out of the blue but someone showed me your post and I wondered if you could give me more details."

Martin told him what had happened. "Sorry to hear that," Sutcliffe replied, "I wonder if you're interested in meeting for a coffee and a chat? I'm interested in writing about your treatment in my column." Martin looked out of the window at the soupy afternoon clouds before replying. "Sure."

*

Henry Sutcliffe sat outside the fancy Marylebone cafe and smoked a cigarette that looked like an extension of himself. His hair was white but, even in his mid-forties, perfectly formed. He was lean under a crisp white shirt and a leather jacket. Martin approached him, feeling three times smaller than he was.

"Martin?" Henry asked, leaping upwards and seizing him by the hand, "So good to meet you, sir. An honour."

"The pleasure is mine," said Martin, with what he liked to imagine was sophistication.

"Sit down! Coffee? Cigarette? I think they have pastries or something..."

Martin sat down and took one of the long, thin cigarettes.

Around them were men in suits and women in tight jackets. Mobile phones rang, beeped and buzzed in an obnoxious symphony. Martin shifted in his chair before settling back. How many of these fuckers had choked out a terrorist? None!

"I was appalled to hear how you have been treated," Henry said, "Appalled. This country. When I think how much people are paid for juggling words and figures and here you are..."

He glanced upwards as if to compose himself.

"It turns my stomach."

Martin shrugged.

"Life."

"It shouldn't be. Here, do you want a coffee? Tell me again what happened."

Martin was halfway through telling the story of his heroism on the tube before he realised that Henry had meant the story of his firing. The journalist listened intently as he talked, though, and made notes in a little black notebook, so he continued before moving on to the events that followed. As he told the story of his meeting with his boss and the flame-haired HR representative, Henry shook his head and clicked his tongue against his teeth.

"Awful. Awful. And all too common. Have you thought about going to an Employment Tribunal?"

"Yeah."

"You will probably lose."

"Oh."

"That is what this country has come to, I'm afraid. But I shall do my best to make your case. Have you thought about writing a book?"

"I haven't even thought about reading one."

Henry exploded into laughter which ended almost as soon as it had begun.

"Well, think about it. I can recommend ghost writers."

The article came out two days later. "Why Do We Neglect Our Heroes and Reward Our Enemies?" was the headline. Martin found himself contrasted with some jihadi (or alleged jihadi) who was suing MI5.

"I found Mr Smith to be a sensitive man with that blunt, charming honesty of the British working class." Sensitive? Where had *that* come from? And he couldn't remember telling Sutcliffe about his "frustration with the government's anti-extremism efforts, or lack thereof, in Britain's educational and cultural institutions." But he was glad to see his name back in the newspapers, and his story in print. He hoped that it had made Paul squirm.

Several other journalists messaged him over that week, asking for statements. Martin was happy to oblige. The questions were slightly odd. What did he think about "wokeness"? He had no idea what is was. It sounded bad.

"Dad's in the paper again sweetheart," he announced to Amanda when she rang him.

"Which this time?"

"The, er – the *American Spectator*..."

"Oh, I read it every day."

He *thought* that she was joking.

"How is it going with jobs?"

"Well," said Martin, ponderously, "I did get an email from a man in Chicago saying I could go to work for him."

"What kind of job?"

"Insurance salesman."

"I think we should focus on England for now, Dad."

Martin sheepishly agreed. After he put the phone down he sat at his kitchen table, listening to the cars outside, as the evening darkened like a bruise.

Henry Sutcliffe had not been reading his DMs. Martin had sent him two - one asking if he had any contacts who might be able to help him find a job and one asking if he had seen the previous message. He knew that he had not. The little tick beside it was still grey.

The next morning, though, his mobile phone sprang to life.

"Martin! Great to hear from you. Henry Sutcliffe here. Are you busy?"

"No."

"I wondered if you might be looking for a job?"

"Yes."

"Perfect. Have you ever heard about the RI? The Raziq Institute. No, probably not. Basically, it is a little organization that promotes secularism and anti-extremism."

"Of course."

"Anyway, I do some work with the lads over there and they have a project that you might be interested in. It's sort of trying to provide a positive, relatable face for moderation. Of course, you will be paid. Interested?"

14

Martin was unsure of what the hell Henry was talking about, but he was curious, and he liked the sound of pay.

"Sure."

"Excellent. Are you free on Wednesday? I'll send the address."

The Raziq Institute was based in Pimlico. Martin found its offices in a grand Georgian building that also appeared to host solicitors, estate agents and a mysterious business called "Wolf Operations". An austere secretary with Slavic features and a suit dress attached to her like clingfilm looked at Martin with deep scepticism before he established exactly who he was. She waved him down a hall which was as sterile and minimalistic as a dental surgery. Arriving at the door that she had motioned to, he knocked.

"Come!"

Martin pushed open the door. Inside was a rather more ramshackle office. Books, folders and loose leaf paper littered the room. This was how Martin imagined universities.

A mouselike man was crouched behind a laptop in a depressing suit. Next to him was a young woman with pinched cheeks and ash blonde hair who Martin recognised as an intern without knowing exactly what an intern was.

"Martin Smith?"

Martin nodded and the man ushered him in and towards a chair. The woman scooped up a book that had been lying on it.

"My name is Robert Norman. Director of Operations. I keep this show on the road."

"Oh," said Martin, trying to sound impressed.

"You've spoken to Henry Sutcliffe, I think? How much did he tell you?"

"*Well*, he said something about, er – something about improving the image of, er – something about a job."

Norman smiled.

"Yes, it *is* about a job, Mr Smith. It's a campaign we're working on and we thought you could help us with."

"A campaign?"

"A campaign for unity. For unity against the extremes of the right *and* left."

"Where do I fit in?"

"We're going to unite people who represent the moderate, sensible, good-humoured spirit of the different communities who make up modern Britain. Muslim Britons. Black Britons. White Britons. People who promote a positive, cohesive, unideological image of our nation."

Martin nodded and scratched his cheek. He still no particular idea of where he fit in, though he suspected that it had something to do with white Britain.

The door opened and two men strolled in. One was a short, lean, nattily dressed Arabic man with a Morrisseyesque quiff and a hipster moustache. The other was a tall, broad-shouldered black man with a crushing handshake and an engaging smile.

"This is Mohamed Badra," Norman said, "Our chairman. And this is Everton Green."

"I'm an author," Green beamed, "*Lives Not Knives.*"

"Great."

"How are you doing Martin," asked Badra, rhetorically, "Are you ready?"

"Ready for what?"

Badra smiled.

"Follow me."

Badra led Martin, Green, Norman and the intern out of the office, down the back of the building and through an exit. He walked out into a grimy back street. Martin began to feel uncomfortable. What was this? Was a sleek black car with tinted windows about to sweep down and whisk them away?

Badra led them round a corner and stopped outside a pub. It was a plush faux-traditional pub, with lots of wood, red velvet and persnickety bar snacks.

"Here we are," he said, brightly.

They walked in. Martin looked around. It had been a long time since he had been in a pub. He saw people smiling, and talking, and laughing. He saw beer, oceans of beer, beer filling glasses, and held in bottles, and gushing from taps.

Badra spoke to a waiter, who led them to a secluded table where a thin young man in a blue t-shirt was setting up a camera.

"Has Norm here let you in on what we're up to Martin?" Badra asked, leaning on the edge of the table, folding his arms and talking in a fast, clipped way that made him sound excited and annoyed at the same time.

"Yeah," said Martin.

Two people had tried to explain it to him and he was still none the wiser. He wondered if that was his fault or theirs.

"It's a podcast," Badra said, "*Drinks in Moderation*. Just a bunch of blokes from different backgrounds meeting over a pint. A bunch of blokes who like football, and banter, and Britain, and dislike extremism and woke nonsense."

Well, that made *some* kind of sense.

"But why me?" asked Martin.

"Because you kicked a terrorist in the nuts," said Badra.

Martin laughed. It had been the nose but never mind.

"Up for it?"

Up for a drink and a chat?

"Sure, why not."

They sat down, with Badra in the middle and Martin and Green on either side of him. The intern put glasses of beer in front of Martin and Green and a glass of Coke in front of Badra.

"Sorry for not drinking," Badra said, breezily, "I never know if God *really* hates drinking but in case He does I'll save my sins for something else."

Martin looked down at the drink.

"Alright guys," said Badra, "Follow my lead. I'll start off with a few questions to get us going. Are we okay with the camera, Norm? I---"

"I don't drink," said Martin.

"Excuse me?"

"I don't drink."

"Don't tell me *you're* a Muslim too."

"I'm an alcoholic."

Badra and Norman looked at one another. Green nodded across the table, silently approving of Martin's resolve.

"God, this isn't good," said Badra, leaning back his chair and sighing as if the weight of the world had fallen on his shoulders, "No offence, Martin. I completely get where you're coming from. But we can't have our salt of the Earth white guy drinking orange juice. What kind of optics is that?"

"I could get some non-alcoholic beer," said Norman.

"That's *worse!*"

"How about I take one of the beer bottles," said the intern, "Empty it and fill it up with water again. He can drink out of the bottle. Nobody would know."

"Brilliant," said Badra, clicking his fingers, "I *knew* there was a reason we kept you around."

The girl smiled and headed for the bar.

"More than one reason," said Badra, watching her leave.

She returned with a beer bottle full of water. Martin tasted it, feeling a strange, familiar hint of alcohol. The young man finished fiddling with the camera and gave a thumbs-up.

"Alright, gentleman," said Norman, "We're going to start with a toast so if you could raise your drinks in the centre of the table."

They did.

"Perfect. On three, you're going to say "cheers" and then we shall begin. One, two, three..."

"Cheers!"

"So, guys," said Badra, launching himself into a question as if they had been chatting for hours, "What do you think about reports that *ISIS* have been *fundraising in London* on behalf of jihadi brides?'

"Well," said Martin, stirring himself into action, "We should find whoever is doing that and kick them out of the country."

"Cut," said Norman, appearing from behind a camera with a look of tolerant disdain, "Uh, Martin, that's not the kind of tone we're going for."

"Oh," said Martin, bemusedly, "Sorry."

Badra frowned as the cameraman prepared himself again. He looked at Green as the young man gave a thumbs-up.

"Well," said Green, "We have to go in there, into those communities, and say, "Look – this ain't on. We aren't going to put up with this. We have to sort it out. We have to do it now.""

"Absolutely," said Badra, "And we need the three Is: intelligence, infiltration, and ideas. Policing is essential. But we have to engage people intellectually as well."

"Yeah," said Martin, *"Of course."*

"We also had reports this morning that British soldiers are being investigated for far right extremism," said Badra, "What do you think, Martin, are there parallels between Jihadis and white supremacists."

"Well, yeah," said Martin, taking a nervous sip of his sparkling water with its twist of Heineken, "I mean they're all fu---well, they're all headbangers aren't they."

"Not very British is it," said Green, cheerfully, "Any kind of extremism I mean."

The conversation stumbled on. Martin did not contribute much except for the odd *yeah* or *sure* or *definitely*. Only when Badra asked a question about the football did Martin summon up the inspiration to say a few words about Gareth Southgate and video assistant referee. When they finished, Badra clapped his hands and nodded.

"Thanks, Martin. Great job."

Green shook his hand.

"Nice meeting you man."

"I'll be in touch about remuneration," Norman said.

"Excuse me?"

"Pay."

Badra and Green had left and Norman and the young man were packing up the camera. Martin drifted out and down the street. He thought he might have done a bad job, and he did not know what to do next. Perhaps Henry Sutcliffe could help. Martin called the journalist. The first time he rang, Sutcliffe did not answer his phone. On the second attempt, he got through and heard his bright Etonian voice.

"Martin, hello."

"Have you got a minute, Henry? I wanted to talk about..."

"You know, this isn't the best time, sadly," said Sutcliffe, "I'm just going to a debate at the Oxford Union. "This house believes that sex is biologically determined." Hot stuff, as you can imagine. I'm in favour, of course. Then I'm meeting with a little group of authors and academics. A *salon* if you will. They want me to talk about my latest book. Very boring, I'm sure. They've said there will be some good booze but I have my doubts."

"Oh," said Martin.

"But I *must* prepare. Can't just wing these things, you know. Much as I'd like to. So, we must catch up later. I'll let you know when I'm free. Whenever that is."

"Sure."

Martin passed another pub. Something about it turned the pavement into glue. It was an unpretentious place: a dingy little boozer where off-white paint peeled off the walls and the sounds of cheers and curses could be heard above the vague crackle of football commentary. Martin peered through the doorway, listening to cheerful clinking of pint glasses. It was like the ringing of church bells. Why not? What not have a drink? He'd found work after all.

Martin pottered in, getting a few suspicious glances from the locals as he approached the bar and ordered a pint of beer and a bag of crisps. The crisps made it seem sensible. He ordered smoky bacon. It was practically a meal.

Martin took his glass and drank. What a drink it was. You never lose your taste for beer. Colleagues, friends, women, all can fade into the mists of time. But you never forget the feeling of an ice cold beer. It transcends all circumstances.

It was so enjoyable that Martin emptied his glass before realising that he was in danger of doing so. He looked at it with disappointment. Well, no harm in one more. He ordered another beer, as well as another bag of crisps. Cheese and onion. Balance.

People were milling benignly around him. Mark Knopfler was crooning on the radio. A woman opposite him had such astounding globular buttocks that he could not help surveying them with scientific curiosity.

But something was wrong. Darkness was setting in.

He remembered his last appearance on TV. It had been on a comedy show, late in 2009. As far as he remembered, it had been a tribute to the noughties – a half-assed attempt to exploit an occasion no one felt especially sad or happy about. He had been asked to stand there, smiling awkwardly, while a parade of gurning comedians tried to remember who he was. They guessed "rugby player", "soldier" and "BNP politician" before the presenter asked him to remind them. The joke was meant to be on *them* but he had felt embarrassed.

Martin felt embarrassed now. What was he doing, talking about "moderation"? He didn't know what it *meant*. It was the sort of word that politicians used to sound respectable – like football managers talking about "consistency" or car salesmen referencing their Italian clients.

He drank his beer and watched as a young woman shook her dreamlike hips. He was getting the backwash now. He was getting the sour dregs of painful memories. He thought about Emma's illness, and how alcohol had colonised the parts of their life not being colonised by cancer. His weakness. He had hated himself for not being able to make her well, but now he hated himself for not being able to make her happy.

Martin finished his pint and ordered another. He took a sip, caught himself, and put it down again, looking at himself in the glass. What the fuck was he doing? It tasted as flat as he felt.

Stomping out of the bar, leaving a trail of baffled expressions in his wake, Martin shambled down the street, feeling foggy and not knowing if it was the alcohol or the emotion.

As he crossed the road, he saw a man and woman lurking in a doorway. Martin slowed. Through the darkness, he could see that the man – dressed in some horrendous sweaty leather jacket – had pinned the young woman against the wall. As Martin approached, he heard raised voices.

"If you ever..."

Martin saw the young man's fingers rising from the woman's arm to her throat.

"Hey!"

The man spun around.

"Leave her alone," Martin told him.

"Mind your fucking busine---"

Martin hit him, straight as a piston, on the nose. Again, he savoured that crunch, so instantly familiar. The man dropped to his knees, but then leapt up again, with drunken valour, and crashed into Martin's chest. Martin threw him against the wall, feeling a nasty twinge in his back, and saw blood leaking from the man's nose and splattering on his shirt and on the street.

"Leave him alone," the woman yelled, but Martin was not listening. The man collected himself and stumbled forwards again, muttering curses. He aimed a punch at Martin and missed, comically and pathetically. Martin

26

grabbed him by the shoulders and tossed him to the ground.

"Get off him!" the woman howled again.

Martin stomped away, leaving the man a bloody, beaten mess. He heard him groaning, and the woman hyperventilating. Even as he left the scene, he could see people looking at him. Glancing down, he realised that his shirt was smeared with blood. He zipped up his jacket and continued. His hand was broken and his back was aching as he barrelled down the street.

His phone rang. It was Amanda.

"Hey Dad!"

"Hey sweetheart."

"We wondered if you wanted to come for dinner at the weekend?"

"Sure, I'd like that."

"Are you outside? You're sounding funny."

"Just been for a run," said Martin, "Thought if I'm not working I can at least do something to improve myself, you know?"

"Ah," Amanda said, "That's good."

"Yeah. Everything is good."

Mental Health

"OH. MY. GAWD."

Ayeesha Phillips spun around, expecting to see blood, or fire, or balaclavas. The scream had torn through the fretful quiet of the supermarket like a bread knife through a blanket.

"AY-EEE-SHAAR!"

A woman was running towards her. She was running in a storm of thick fake fur - a pink tornado. One of her hands was keeping a wide-brimmed hat balanced on her head and the other was clutching a spiky red handbag.

The storm arrived. Thin arms emerged and flung themselves around Ayeesha's neck.

"Tina?"

"You fuckin' bet. How are ya, love?"

"I'm okay. How are you?"

Tina McClaine stepped back, releasing Ayeesha from her grip. Her face, under the hat, looked even smaller than it was, especially when framed by curtains of long, off-blonde hair. Her eyes were sparkling.

"Oh, you know me love!"

She did?

"I haven't seen you in *ages*!" Tina said, "Not since..."

"The reunion," Ayeesha said, stepping in to save her old friend's floundering memory, "Six years ago."

"God, we're *old*," said Tina, "You know, I don't remember that party at all."

"You got quite drunk."

"Sounds like me, darlin'."

Tina leaned in closer, conspiratorially.

"Not now though. Six months sober."

"Congrats."

An awkward silence fell. Ayeesha was still too bewildered to know what to say. Tina looked as if she had surprised herself with her own excitement. She stood there for a moment, opening and closing her mouth like a fish pressing itself against the side of its bowl.

"Oh, Christ," she said, suddenly, "My shopping."

They hurried together to the end of the aisle, where Tina had left her trolley. It was sitting, horizontally, in the middle of the aisle. Shoppers inched around it with silent grimaces. Ayeesha glanced inside. There were two green smoothies, a tub of cottage cheese and an energy drink. Tina gripped the trolley proprietorially.

"Right," she said, "Now I've got you, love, I'm not going to let you go. You're coming for coffee."

"But my shopping," said Ayeesha.

"There's a cooler in my car."

Ayeesha looked at her phone. She had an hour before she was meant to be home. Her mum was sitting with her kids while she went to the hairdressers, Tesco and the garage. Her car would have to wait.

"Okay."

"Awesome! Come on."

They bought their things, stashed them away in the back of Tina's car and crossed the street to Starbucks. A couple of passers-by looked at Tina as she bustled in. Ayeesha ordered a latté and Tina ordered an Americano.

"Caffeine," she gasped, impersonating an addict.

They sat at the furthest end of the room, with Tina facing the door. She looked around for any signs of recognition and sipped her coffee, wrapping her all but fleshless fingers around the sides of the mug.

"So, what have you been doing, love?"

"Well, my kids are four and six," Ayeesha said.

"Get *out* of here," Tina said, punching Ayeesha in the arm with a little too much force, "I thought you had one kid. Are you still married?"

"Yes."

"Good going. Wow, look at you! Got everything together."

Tina's voice dipped, almost imperceptibly, towards a note of sadness.

"And how are you?"

"Good," said Tina, brightening, "Back on TV."

"I saw."

"Have you watched me? It's a series about my mental health journey, you know? Of course, it's not as fun as when we were all in the house. Those were the days. Drinking, dancing and shagging fit blokes under a big pile of blankets."

Ayeesha remembered. She hadn't fucked anyone. That would have been too far. Still, she remembered getting out of the house and seeing a big photo of her french kissing Tina next to a report about two soldiers dying in Iraq. Her father hadn't spoken to her for years.

"I want to do some good with this series, though," said Tina, worrying the corners of her hair, "You know, I hit the *bottom*. I was an alcoholic. A drug addict. I was depressed. I'd lost my husband. I'd lost my mum. I'd lost my career. I want people to see that if *I* can get help *they* can as well."

"That's great! Good for you."

"You were always more sensible than me, love," laughed Tina, "We were the crazy girls in that series but for you it was a phase and for me it was natural."

Ayeesha was not so sure. She had been startled when she had emerged from the Big Brother house to find herself the subject of national intrigue. The tabloids could not get enough of the Muslim schoolgirl who had rebelled against her parents and become a wild child. The broadsheets had carried articles with headlines like "The British Media's Treatment of Ayeesha Ali Shows the True Power of Orientalism". A lad's mag had asked for a topless photo shoot. Ayeesha knew she could have pushed it into a career. She could have been an earlier, softer version of the lady who had sucked cock in a hijab. But she didn't want it. She was viscerally repulsed by the thought of being used by strangers for masturbatory purposes – literal or intellectual.

"So, you're doing better?"

"There's better and *better* ain't there," said Tina, "I've been doing a *lot* of work. Counselling. Therapy. Meditation. CBD."

"CBT?"

"Hm? No, the oil. You know, I've been connecting with my childhood and everything that happened in the house and after it. I'm feeling good."

"I'm happy for you," Ayeesha said, touching Tina's arm.

"Can I tell you something though?"

"Sure!"

"I'm scared."

"What?"

Tina looked around and lowered her voice.

"I'm scared."

"Why?"

Tina was blushing behind a wall of foundation.

"Well I've got this mental health series right."

"Yes."

"All about my mental illness."

"Yeah."

"So, what if I get better?"

"What?"

"What if I get *better*? You know this whole series is about me being mentally ill. If I get better I'm not interesting anymore. What am I going to talk about? How good I feel? Who wants that?"

"You've got other talents, babe."

"The fuck I do," laughed Tina, merrily, "My talent – my one talent – is being a massive fuck-up."

She shook her head.

"How are the kids, love?"

Ayeesha told Tina about how her eldest was obsessed with Lego, and how she was scared about him getting into video games and YouTube, and she told her about how her youngest had been so quiet that they had been concerned that her brain was not developing. Tina nodded studiously as if Ayeesha was trying to explain nuclear physics.

They went outside for a cigarette.

"God, it's cold," said Tina, wrapping her arms around herself.

It wasn't.

As Tina ground her cigarette out on the edge of a bin, two girls in crop tops sauntered by. One of them stopped. She looked at Tina and her eyes bulged.

"Oh my Gawd, are you Tina McClaine?"

"That's me love," grinned Tina.

"Oh my *Gawd*," said the girl, flapping her hands and hyperventilating, "I *love* your show. It's helped me *so* much."

"That makes my day."

Tina snapped a cheerful selfie with the girls and watched them bustle off, nattering to one another. She looked back at Ayeesha, half happy and half wistful.

"No, I can't get better," she said, "I *can't* get better."

Ayeesha drove home. She unlocked the door, headed to the kitchen and put her lukewarm products into the fridge. She exchanged a few words with her mum before seeing her off. Their relationship was better now but it was never warm. She had thought that getting married and having kids would prove herself as a daughter but it had not been enough.

She wondered where Mick was. In a business meeting or out at the bar? She could hear her son playing in his bedroom and her daughter watching cartoons in the lounge. She opened the cupboard in the corner of the kitchen and reached behind the saucepans to extract a bottle of vodka. Filling the cap, she threw the liquid down her throat and then quickly replaced the bottle, feeling warmth spread through her body.

Ayeesha stood up and leaned against the counter top. Outside, in the garden, the tree was blooming. Fluffy blossom rested on its limbs. It would die soon. But not that day.

No Gods, No Masters

What's up guys. This is No Gods, No Masters. That's right, it's your boy, NGNM, back with another video. It's been a while.

I think I just lost motivation, you know. Back in the day I had tens of thousands of people watching me. Now, if I want to break five figures I have to put Jordan Peterson in the thumbnail. I don't *care* about Jordan Peterson.

What *do* I care about? I'm not sure. I cared about a lot of things back in the day. Most of all, I care about making videos. That and weed. When I started making videos it was the best thing ever. It was *better* than weed. Every morning I woke up and asked myself what I was going to talk to you guys about.

It wasn't just the views. It was - how can I put this without sounding like an asshole - it was important. It *felt* important. It was 2008. Saying there was no God still felt amazing. It felt radical. Now it feels like saying the sky is blue.

It was a different time. And it was exciting to have a place to express yourself. It was, er, organic. It hadn't been swallowed by the mainstream. It felt like there was no massive difference between Richard Dawkins, Christopher Hitchens and *me*. We were all part of the same movement. We were peers.

And everything seemed so obvious. Have you ever seen a burning bush? Have you ever seen a glass of water turn into a glass of wine? People talk about Aquinas and Augustine but when I was a kid religion was Jerry Falwell telling you that gays caused 9/11. What was I supposed to think?

It was dumb. It was all dumb. But at least it was real. It was real people saying what they really thought. Then people worked out how to make money from the platform and you know what happened then. Our little skate park turned into a shopping mall.

People were bored of arguing about God. I get it. You can't have the same debate over and over again. But instead of *everyone* talking about religion *everyone* started to talk about social justice. I did as well. People watched if I talked about feminism. No one would have watched if I had talked about, er, woodworking.

I talked about MRAs. I talked about MGTOW. I talked about incels. I don't remember what half of these things were. What is an MRA? It sounds like something you would wear condoms to avoid. But I talked about it.

I've been thinking while I've been offline...

I know my hair is a mess, by the way. I should have got it cut before I made a "comeback" but I never got around to it. I know I've lost weight as well. I don't think I'm eating less. Perhaps I'm sick. Perhaps I'm dying. should get a blood test.

What was I talking about? Oh yeah. I've been thinking while I've been offline. I've been thinking about --- my *thoughts*.

That sounds gay, I know. I mean, that sounds lame. But I've been thinking about how my thoughts have changed.

It's like I'm thinking for an audience. It's like I'm performing. I go into a store, or to a park, or to McDonald's, and I have this *commentary*. This *babble*.

I can't just wonder about people and things, or even ignore them, I need to have *opinions*. "When did guys start wearing flip flops in public?" That kind of thing. And I'm not just commenting on other people. I'm commenting on myself. You know, I look in the mirror and I hear this voice saying, "Look at this guy's skin, you could cook a burger on his face."

I was seeing a girl and all the time that we were going at it I could hear, "This is terrible. What is this? Are they having sex or a seizure? I can't get hard to this."

It's like it isn't even me! It's someone else. It's *something* else. If I want to have a break from it I have to listen to music really loud. *Really* loud. Slayer or something. I have to do a *lot* of drugs.

I can hear it now. "What does this idiot think he's doing? Does he think anyone cares? Or is he talking to himself? Is that camera even on?"

The Joke

Leaning back and sipping whisky in the comfort of the VIP section, Jack Munro felt as if he had reached the mountain top. After years of slogging round comedy clubs and local theatres, he had burst into the mainstream, on panel shows, on game shows and finally with his hit series *Jack of All Trades*.

Jack looked round the club, taking in a sea of legs. He was only 36. Ricky Gervais had been 39 when he had made *The Office*. Now look at him! Jack had reached *a* mountain top, in other words, but perhaps there were more peaks to conquer. "You could make a film Jack," his agent had told him, "You could crack America! You could host the Oscars!"

Jack felt his bladder lurch. He went to cross the room, but two pairs of sparkling sea-blue eyes and sweetly sloping breasts stood in his way. He looked at the women before him.

"Are you Jack Munro?"

"Yeah."

"Can we have a selfie?"

"Sure."

Jack smiled as the young women draped themselves around him. He hoped it was a smile and not a leer. Oh *God* he wanted to stay and talk to the girls but he had made an appointment with the urinal and he could not afford to miss it. There would be girls again.

Edging his way through the bodies and the smoke, Jack slipped into the bathroom, where the smell of piss and sweat was almost thick enough to cut. He approached a urinal, released himself and let fly, dousing a wad of gum that had been stuck to the ceramic. When he turned around, a man was stood in front of him.

"Woah."

The man was tall, and thin enough to make cyclists look like strongmen. He wore a leather jacket and the sleeves hung around his wrists like lampshades.

"Mr Munro?"

"What?"

"I want to talk to you."

"Here!?"

Jack did up his zip.

"It's about your career."

"Call my agent."

"I don't think you want anyone else to hear this."

Jack looked at him carefully. He knew the man was probably a bullshit artist but he was curious. Besides, if the man wanted trouble he was sure that even *he* could beat him up. He motioned towards a stall and they went inside, standing face to face, inches from each other.

"I have information," said the man, "That you might not want other people to have."

Jack exploded into laughter.

"You're going to blackmail me? Mate, half of my act is about how I am a fucking loser who has ruined every relationship I've ever had. I have a joke about getting the clap. I have a joke about needing to sneeze mid-cunnilingus. I have a joke about shitting myself at the Royal Albert Hall. What are you going to say that I haven't already said?"

The man took out his phone in silence and played an audio file. Jack recognised his voice. It was crackly, as if it had been recorded years before, but it was definitely him. He was talking on stage, interacting with the audience. Somebody was heckling him.

Then he heard the joke.

It was not a scripted joke. It was spontaneous. He heard the audience groan and gasp and then he heard himself hurriedly moving on with his set.

"Come on, mate," he stammered, "That was years ago. I must have been twenty."

"You're on social media," smiled the man, "Do you think that matters?"

He played the joke again. *That* joke. With *those* words. Jack made a series of noises to encourage the man to turn off the clip. He could feel his heart sinking down his chest, past his waist, down his leg and into his shoe. The man was still smiling at him.

"Where did you get this?" Jack asked.

"I collect things," said the man, "That's my business. But if I post this on Twitter then it will be *your* business."

"So, what do you want?"

"Ten thousand pounds," said the man, cold and businesslike, "You're going to lose a lot more than that if this leaks online. Bring it here at 10:00 PM on Wednesday. If you bring the cops then it will come out, I promise you."

Jack nodded dumbly as the man passed him a card with an address written on it. He thought about the lost money, and the lost friends, and the lost opportunities. The man straightened his jacket, opened the door and walked out of the stall. Another man was stood outside and looked at them with bafflement.

"Business meeting," said the man as he left the toilets.

Jack, the comedian, had no idea what to say.

At home, Jack keeled over onto a chair. He tried to find some humour in the situation. Here he was, being blackmailed not because of hidden crimes or furtive sexual deviance but because of a joke. A joke! It was absurd! It was an objectively funny thing to happen to him. Jack tried to laugh and let out a little sob.

Perhaps he could get ahead of the story? Admit he made the joke, apologise and explain what was happening to him. People might sympathise. They might forgive him.

Jack heard the joke echoing around his head. No, they would not forgive him.

He imagined the joke being released on Twitter. "Yikes," someone would say. "Oof," another would add. "Hey, @Channel4," another would declare, "You okay having this piece of shit working for you?" Replies, retweets, and quote tweets would multiply like cancer cells inside a doomed man's body. Insults, condemnations and expressions of surprise and disappointment would be united in a seething, pulsing mass which would slither out of the screen and secure itself around Jack's face.

Nor could he go to the police. The story would leak out somehow. He knew that perfectly well from an unfortunate argument he had had with his ex-girlfriend. He *could* just pay but could he trust that that would fix the situation? They could take the cash and sell the story to the papers nonetheless.

Jack called his manager.

"Stefan?" he asked tentatively, "You know you worked with that MMA fighter?"

"Duke," his manager said, "He's a psychopath."

"You thought he was working in organised crime?"

"Yeah. Why?"

"Have you got his number?"

Stefan paused.

"Do you have some kind of problem, Jack?"

"No," Jack laughed, putting all of his nascent acting skills to the test, "It's for the next series. Gavin thinks we should have some edgier jobs next time so I thought I could see if this guy is interested. He sounds charismatic."

"Oh, he's *charismatic*," Stefan said, dubiously, "Okay, here it is. But don't sign a contract for the next series. We're holding out for a raise, right?"

Jack looked around his flat. It never failed to amaze him that he had a flat. Not a shared flat. Not a rented flat. A flat *he had. In London.* Just three years before he had been dealing with two crazy flatmates and a crazier landlord. If he had no work he would have to move out again. Never mind films and famous friends. He could wave goodbye to thoughts of marriage and starting a family. Being 36 suddenly seemed very old.

Jack called Duke.

"Yeah?"

The voice on the other side of the line sounded simultaneously uninterested and annoyed.

"This is Jack Munro. I got your number from Stefan Kowalski."

"And?"

"I've got a job for you."

"What job?"

"Should we talk about it here?"

There was silence.

"Give me your address," Duke said, "I'll be there at eight."

Jack remembered that he had a date that night. It didn't seem like a good idea to disagree with Duke. Besides, he didn't feel much like sex *or* steak. He gave him his address.

Duke arrived at 9 on the dot. He had craggy features and a handshake that could turn flesh and bone to pulp. He wore a bomber jacket that had clearly seen some things and a watch which could have blinded you if it had caught the light.

"Nice place," he said, looking around like a debt collector.

"Drink?"

"Nah."

Jack hesitated as Duke turned a look towards him that could have frozen the body of a freshly butchered cow.

"Well," he said, "The job is this: a man has information I don't want people to have, and he wants some money for it."

"So?"

"Well," Jack repeated, swallowing dry air, "I've heard that you fix problems and I thought you could fix this one."

Duke nodded.

"You want him to disappear."

"What? No. God. No! I just want you to scare him."

Duke nodded, his features still. He looked around the flat again.

"You got this place by telling jokes?"

"There's more to it than that," said Jack, hesitantly.

"Like?"

"Well, I have to *write* the jokes. I, er – I go to meetings."

Duke nodded his silent, stony nod.

Making people laugh had been easier before. A joke had just been a joke. Jack had made all the 9/11 jokes, and all the dead baby jokes, and all the semi-ironic women jokes. He wasn't sure if he should feel ashamed morally but he felt bad comedically. None of the jokes had been very good. He had relied on the audience enjoying their sense of themselves as unshockable. Now they were more liable to enjoy a sense of themselves as being smart and good. How *funny* Jack was being was almost irrelevant.

He had worked hard to fit in with the times. He had made all the UKIP jokes, and all the Brexit jokes, and all the Trump jokes. Stefan had told him he was vulnerable, being male, pale and stale. Jack had worked on a whole bit about how being ginger put him in a marginalised group – the crux of which was that girls in his school had slept with people regardless of the colour of their skin but would discriminate against the colour of their hair – but Stefan had firmly recommended its exclusion.

Jack's phone rang as he lay in bed.

"Mr Munro?"

It was the man from the club.

"What."

"There's no need to have that attitude, Mr Munro."

"Do you have to talk like a Bond villain? How did you get my number anyway?"

"That's my business," said the man, sounding a bit offended, "I just wanted to remind you about Wednesday."

"I haven't forgotten."

"And I wanted to remind you not to involve the police. I'm not the only one with the file Jack. You wouldn't want it leaking out, would you?"

"I'll be there."

He would. But he wouldn't be alone.

Jack was slipping into an appropriately dark hoodie when his phone rang. He assumed that it would be Duke or his blackmailer and felt mingled shock and consternation when he heard that it was Stefan.

"Jack! How are you?"

"Great," said Jack, wondering he should take a knife.

"Look, sorry to disturb you but a job has come up. A film. An American film. They want a sort of cheeky chappy English actor."

"So, I'll do it."

"It's an action film, Jack. Do you think you're up for action?"

"Sure," said Jack, zipping his hoodie up.

"Great. I'll send you the details of the audition tomorrow. It could be a big break, Jack."

The man had told Jack to meet him on a gloomy corner of a park near Winchmore Hill. Duke had told Jack he would be following him. Act normal, he had said, as if there was a normal way of acting when you were paying off a blackmailer's demands. Jack walked around a pond, gazing into its muddy depths, and wondered what Duke's plan was. He had asked him just to scare the man. It had seemed disrespectful to ask how he would do it. Duke was the professional after all.

Jack saw a tree in the distance and headed off across the grass. He could feel the money in his pocket. It had a strange, unnatural heft. He wondered if the wad of notes was thick enough to stop a bullet.

The man was stood underneath a tree, and in the autumn chill looked wiry enough to be one. He had a dark blue raincoat on, with the hood pulled over his face.

"Came alone?"

"No," sneered Jack, "I've got the fucking paratroopers with me. Don't you want your money?"

The man frowned and nodded. Jack told himself not to get cocky. Taking out the envelope that contained the notes, he weighed it in his palm.

"How do I know you're going to delete the file?"

"I can send you a video of it being deleted."

"How do I know you haven't got another?"

The man sighed.

"You don't."

Jack felt the wind biting through his jacket. There was silence. He handed the money over. There was nothing else to do.

"Thank you."

Where was Duke?

"Aren't you going to count it?"

"Eh?"

"Aren't you going to count it? I mean, you don't know if that's the right amount."

The man looked flustered.

"It would be quite dumb of you t---"

He dropped to the ground. Duke was standing behind him in his bomber jacket and a balaclava. He held a pistol in his hand. He must have cracked the man behind the ear with the handle.

Jack froze. Duke pulled the man up from the grass and shoved him against the tree. Holding the gun he held it against the man's mud smeared brow. The man's eyes had inflated and his mouth was hanging open. Duke audibly sneered.

"Listen, cunt," he said, "Here is what we're going to do. You're going to call your little friends and tell him to delete whatever they have on this man. If they don't then you and they are *fucked*. Understand?"

Duke placed the gun between the man's open lips and he nodded frantically. Duke removed the gun and the man scrambled for his phone and desperately found a contact.

"It's me," he said, panting, "Delete it. *Just delete it.*"

"Well done," said Duke, taking the phone, "We'll be keeping this. If we hear another word from you then you and anybody on this phone is in trouble. Got it?"

"Got it."

Duke smashed him in the face with his elbow.

"Come on," Jack said, "I think..."

Duke was not listening. He threw the man away from the tree, aiming a neat kick at his backside as he fell across the grass. The man scrambled to his feet and staggered off. Duke picked the money up.

"I think half of this is mine," he said, politely.

As they sat in the car, Jack struggled to control his breathing. He put his hands against the wheel to steady them.

"One question," said Duke, "What did he have on you? Been fucking around? Drug stuff? Worse?"

"No," said Jack.

"Then what?"

He sighed.

"It was a joke."

"A joke? You brought me here over a joke?"

"It was a bad one," said Jack, "An offensive one. I made it years ago and he'd recorded it."

"Go on."

"I don't think..."

Duke twitched as if he was about to detonate.

"I said *go on*."

Jack sighed, explained the context and told the joke. Duke raised his eyebrows and shook his head. He looked as if he could not quite believe what he was hearing.

"Fuck me, mate," he said, with a whistle, "Why would you *say* that?"

"It was years ago," protested Jack, "It was a different time."

"*Still...*"

Duke shook his head and wiped blood off his sleeve.

"I'm no saint should have a word with yourself mate. Be better, yeah?"

*

At home, Jack felt dim with an emotion on the borderlands between embarrassment and guilt. He went onto Twitter and posted noisily in defence of trans rights. Whatever neither he nor his blackmailers knew was that a bomb was ticking beneath his very nose. It was a tweet, from 2010. *That* kind of tweet. With *those* words.

By Grand Central Station I Sat Down and Slept

Edward Julius Courtenay woke up before his wife and bustled into the kitchen to make her coffee. Edward was an early riser. He had to be to get to work in central New York. Anastasia walked in behind him. They hugged in an awkward angular embrace.

Crying erupted. Frederick was awake. Edward marched into his bedroom scooped him out of his cot and held him in the air with a tender awww. Anastasia fondly watched her husband and her son.

Edward got dressed, picked up his briefcase and went to work with a cheerful goodbye. Anastasia fed their son and went to have a shower. As she scrubbed her armpits, she sang, "Bish ka zor, ka zor."

Ella saw that it was 7:30. She closed the game and turned off the computer. For a moment, she could see her face in the screen: puffy, pale and frowning.

As she left the flat to go to work, Ella almost collided with her neighbours's child. She looks down, flustered, as the little boy looked up at her with big blue eyes. His mum dashed out of their flat, seizing him by the hand, and smiled apologetically at Ella.

"Always lose the keys," she panted, before bustling off with her son complaining in her wake.

Ella frowned. The woman and her husband always seemed to be in some kind of hurry. They should do something about their time management, she reflected. It had to be hard on their son.

At work, Ella fixed a swimming pool-sized coffee and began to answer emails. There was, she thought, an artificial quality to her work. She had no contact with the products that her company produced, or the money that sailed in its thousands between accounts. She had never met most of the people she spoke with. When she had been working at home, during the pandemic, it had made little difference.

All that she had missed was office gossip. Serena was in a bad mood because her husband had stayed in bed all Sunday with a hangover.

"Don't put up with that," Ella told her, "If you let him then he'll be a kid forever."

"I feel like it's always me making the effort," sniffed Serena, picking nervously at breadsticks.

"You have to think about yourself," Ella said, taking a bite of vinegary spinach, "Especially if *he* won't."

"He's a good guy."

"Sure."

At home, Ella sank into a packet of biscuits and returned to her game. She was renovating Edward and Anastasia's house, turning the spare room into a gym. She had thought about making it a games room but the couple needed exercise and she was not going to let Edward be childish enough to have a "mancave".

Ella could hear the neighbours's son screaming. What did they *do* to that child? For an absurd moment, she worried that he was going to wake up Frederick.

Edward Julius Courtenay was an architect. He had designed a handsome library in the middle of New York, which had, at his insistence, also been employed to offer free classes for ex-convicts and childcare for single mothers.

Anastasia was a human rights lawyer. They had met at some appalling black tie dinner, where both of them had been equally bored and disgusted. They had taken off together, to a dive bar, and before the night had finished, according to a well-received short story that Ella had uploaded to an erotic fiction site, *"his cock was raising rainforests from her fertile earth."*

Ella closed the computer and went for a bath. The skin of her thighs and wrists groaned as she touched them. She dragged the flannel slowly across her stomach and looked up at the glowing lights fixed to the ceiling.

Back in her room, Ella lay on her bed and looked at the app. One of her conversations had spluttered to a halt when the man had said that vegetarians "just need a whiff of bacon and they'll come around." Another man had opened with "hey butiful". Ella felt a bit guilty ignoring him. At least he had been civilised enough not to send her, as another had, a photo of his button mushroom genitals. But it was far from being her first trip around the block. She knew how it went. She had a lot of choice, yes, but a lot of choice between different shades of awkward sex and disappointing conversation. She closed the app and sank into sleep.

Ella woke up suddenly, jerked from unconsciousness by a commotion that died down so quickly that she did not have enough time to locate its source. What had it been? Some sort of crash? Stumbling out into the corridor, she heard low voices from the neighbouring flat.

Had something happened to the child? Or perhaps an argument had turned physical. Or perhaps a photograph had fallen off the wall. Who knew. Ella returned to uninspiring dreams.

"He said he was sorry," said Serena on Tuesday morning.

"Talk is cheap," said Ella.

"Yes, I know, but he also got me flowers, and wine, and chocolate. He was *so* sweet."

Flowers, and wine and chocolate were pretty cheap as well, thought Ella, unless this idiot was buying orchids and champagne. Whatever. She would see his real face in time.

"Hey."

The message hit her DMs that afternoon.

"Haven't I seen you somewhere?"

56

"I don't know," said Ella, "Have you?"

"I don't know," he said, "I'll have to see you in real life to check."

It *wasn't* subtle. It *wasn't* funny. But she liked it.

"You have my attention," she wrote.

"Could I take it out for dinner?"

Ella sighed. She looked at his photos. There was potential here. Muscles lurked beneath a comfortable layer of fat. His dress sense looked like it needed a few tweaks instead of an exhaustive and exhausting overhaul. He still had hair. This was a body in its 30s that you could *improve* rather than watch gracelessly decline. True, he was not the most handsome man in the world but she was not arrogant enough to think that she was its most gorgeous woman.

The man, Graham, had invited her to Mario's. It was a nice restaurant – not the nicest, perhaps, but a nice one. Ella told herself that it was possible that Graham could afford the nicest restaurant but did not want to be too dramatic on a first date.

On the night, she wore makeup sparingly. She did not want to look too interested. Still, she curled her hair and wore a dress that showed off *just* enough cleavage. After all, she did not want to look *un*interested.

Graham was sitting at a table in the corner of the restaurant. He was wearing a nice jacket and clean shoes,

57

and when he leaned in to kiss Ella on the cheek she caught a pleasant whiff of aftershave. With his strong jaw and clear eyes he was what might have been called "daytime television handsome", even with his moderate paunch and slightly rectangular head.

"I never know what to say first," he laughed.

"You could ask me what I want to drink?"

"I've already ordered wine."

"Red? Sweet?"

"White. Dry.

"Good. I *hate* sweet wines."

She ordered risotto and he did as well, saying that he trusted her judgement when it came to food. Panic lunging across his features, he clarified that this was because "cooking" had been among her interests on the app. Ella laughed and filed it as a "don't know" on her mental list of his good and bad qualities.

Still, they had a nice meal. Graham asked her questions and was either interested or very good at pretending to be interested.

He read. He liked to travel, and not just to Paris or Ibiza but to more interesting places like Singapore. He claimed to really care about the environment.

"So, why do you do so much flying?"

"Well," said Graham, "I don't think we can blame individuals. I think we have to the *system*."

Ella nodded. It seemed like a good point.

"Do you have plans for Christmas?"

"Not yet," Ella shrugged, "We'll see..."

Graham reached out and took her hand. Ella smiled and cocked her head as he wrapped his strong, firm fingers around hers. It was a rather forward gesture. But it seemed romantic as he looked into her eyes and smiled.

Unless...

Graham's smile broadened as he pulled Ella's hand closer towards him and pressed it against his crotch. Ella pulled her hand back and it popped out of his grip. His mouth fell open as her eyes aimed lasers deep into his soul.

"I'm sorry..."

"Yeah."

"I misunderstood..."

"Sure."

Ella stood and gathered up her things. She turned around and started walking from the restaurant, leaving her spoon planted in the middle of the shattered crème brûlée. As she left she passed a waiter carrying a bottle of sparkling wine.

Climbing the stairs to her apartment, Ella heard the kid screaming again. She could hear the mum and dad talking in raised voices as well, though she could not make out what they were saying.

Bella Hastings was an award winning novelist. She lived in a small, elegant house in Notting Hill with her partner, Samantha. They lived with their two dogs and spent their weekends touring flea markets and second-hand bookshops.

That morning, as it was Friday, Bella poured herself a tall glass of white wine to sip as she worked.

The door rang. Ella frowned, walked over and looked through the peephole. It was her neighbours. Ella opened the door warily. The woman had red, puffy eyes, as if she had been crying. The man looked as if he had seen a poltergeist.

"We had a visit from child services," the woman said.

"Oh?"

"We haven't *done* anything."

"That's really not my busine---"

"Do you know anything about this?"

"Has anyone *said* anything?"

"I haven't *heard* anything," said Ella.

"No?"

"I'm sure it's just a big misunderstanding," said Ella, "If you haven't done anything..."

The woman nodded slowly. Ella closed the door.

Bella leaned back in her chair and sipped her glass of wine. She thought about a terrible case that her friend had been discussing. The Courtenays, a family of three in New York, had been found dead when a fire had spread rapidly through their home. Inexplicably, their door had failed to open. Bella's friend saw some morbid comedy in the fact that Mr Courtenay was an architect. Bella thought the case was moving, though, as well as tragic. Imagine how much more sad it would have been if one parent had survived. At least they had died together. There was some romance in that.

Potential

Terry Malcolm dropped his shopping bags onto the back seat of his car and watched, as if in slow motion, as they toppled over and sent products spilling messily across the floor.

Sighing, he clambered in and bent over as far as his ageing joints would allow, scooping up tomatoes and cans of Diet Coke. A bottle of ketchup was lying underneath the front seat. Terry was doing his best to lean that extra inch forwards when he heard someone opening the door of his car. He froze.

"Fam, this one's open!"

"Serious?"

Someone opened the other door and through the space between the front seats Terry saw two men jump into the car. He popped up.

"What the fuck?"

Everybody in the car seemed to say it in the unison. Before Terry could work out what was happening he saw that two long, thin, serrated knives were pointed at his throat. The two men were wearing black coats, hoods and balaclavas.

"What are you doing?"

Again, everyone seemed to speak as one.

"It's my car," said Terry, who had the best answer.

The two men paused, as if trying to make sense of the situation. One of them was short and squat while his friend was tall and lean.

"Let's go," said the taller man, withdrawing his knife.

"Nah."

The shorter, fatter man looked back at Terry and edged his knife further towards his neck.

"Get out."

Terry thought about it. Good sense told him to get out and run. It was just a car. But he was a stubborn bastard. He had a sneaking sense that if he left the vehicle his retreat would haunt him every night he spent alone in his flat. He found it hard to get over his football team losing a match so he would never forget acquiescing to thieves.

"No."

"You fucking mad?"

The man turned to his friend for support but the taller man was gazing out of the window, across the car park, perhaps to see if anyone was coming.

"I'm not kidding, bruv," spat the shorter man, "Get out."

Terry noticed that the taller, thinner man had been looking at him strangely – strangely, that is, inasmuch as his stare was *not* aggressive. The shorter, stockier young man had wild bloodshot eyes. The taller, thinner man looked awkward. His eyes were darting around. He looked as if he would prefer to be somewhere else.

"I'm going to give you five seconds," said the first man, breathing heavily through his nose like an irate rhinoceros, "To get out of this car."

"No."

The pair looked at him incredulously.

"It's my fucking car!" Terry reminded them.

"You can get the money back on insurance," said the second man, almost apologetically.

"It's not about the money, it's my fucking car!"

"Quiet bruv."

"I WILL NOT BE QUIET WHEN YOU ARE TRYING TO STEAL MY CAR."

The shorter, more aggressive man lunged forward with his knife but the taller, nervous man held him back and looked at Terry.

"Quiet Terry," he said, hushing him.

Terry stopped.

"What did you say?"

The young man shrank back as his friend wheeled around to turn a startled gaze towards him.

"Bruv, you *know* this guy?"

"Nah," said the taller man, looking out of the window again.

As the young man turned, the top of his head dipped towards Terry. Instinctively, Terry bent forwards, grabbed the top of his balaclava and pulled it off his head. The young man slapped his hand over the bottom of his face but Terry had already recognised him.

"Jesus Christ," he said, "Liam Okafor."

"How ya doing, coach," said the young man sullenly.

The fatter man looked like he wanted to stab Terry, but he also looked like he was tempted to stab his friend if he did not get some answers. He pulled his balaclava further down his face with one hand and waved his knife with the other.

"Someone tell me what is going on," he said.

"I was Liam's football coach," said Terry, "Years ago."

"I didn't know it was your car," frowned Liam, fidgeting like a naughty schoolboy.

"He was the best player in his year," snapped Terry, serving up a grievance he had been fermenting ever since he had seen Liam's 18-year-old face in an article about drug dealing, "Strong. Quick. Great technique. You went to play with Reading. What the fuck happened?"

Liam shrugged.

"No one could drive me to training."

"Eh?"

"No one could drive me to training."

"What? That's the reason? You could have asked me!"

"Really?" Liam smiled.

"You could have *asked*."

"Yeah, well," Liam shrugged again, "Everything happens for a reason."

"Are we going to take this car or not," snapped the other man, who was clearly feeling left out of the conversation.

"Nah," said Liam, grimacing, "I mean, he's seen me, hasn't he."

"He's also seen you get into his car and stick a knife in his face, fam."

"You won't snitch will you, Terry?"

Terry was still looking down the blade of a knife.

"No."

"Serious?"

"I said no!"

Liam's friend was unhappy. Smoke was practically emanating from his balaclava as he breathed in and out.

"We can't trust this guy."

"Nah," said Liam, "He's okay."

Terry looked at Liam as the other man pocketed his knife dubiously.

"You'll cut this shit out, won't you, Liam?"

"Sure, coach," said Liam, smiling a rueful smile that turned into a little sneer as he slipped his balaclava down over his face.

Terry drove home with shaking hands. He parked around the back of his building and looked up and down the yard to see if anyone was there. As he retrieved his bags from the back of his car he noticed that he had stamped on his bottle of tomato ketchup – spraying its dark red contents across the bottom of his car.

At home, Terry dropped into a chair. He looked at the cupboard beneath the television and thought for a moment. Standing up, with a heavy sigh, he stumbled forwards and opened the door. Inside was a stack of documents that had been idly assembled over the years. Underneath them all was a little plastic bag.

Terry rolled a spliff. He remembered a football match, years before. Liam had been meant to take a free kick. It had been perfectly situated, on the edge of the penalty box, to the left of the net. As he had run forward to take it, though, his foot had slipped on the sweaty grass and he had dragged the ball wide.

A boy on the other team had laughed. It was natural. Not for Liam, though. He had walked forward, his features unmoving, and driven his head into the young boy's face. The boy's nose had been splattered like an overripe strawberry. God knows how but Terry had explained it away as an accident.

Terry rolled the spliff between his fingers and peered into the deep black screen of the television.

"He's okay." So, who wouldn't be okay? The next old man who had done no harm to anyone? A young boy coming home from school? A woman? Would they be okay?

Signing and rubbing his brow, Terry took out his mobile and dialled 999.

"Hello? I've been threatened with a knife. Yes. Yes. I'm at home. Yeah, sure, I can stay on hold."

Terry looked at the documents lying on the floor. Inside two fat folders were copies of the "football CVs" his players had written to send off to scouts. Opening one of them, he found the sticker marked "2009" and rifled through the papers. There it was: "Liam Okafor, 11".

I'm good at passing. Good at shooting. Team player. Always listen to my coach. One day I'll be a pro.

"Mr Malcolm? Are you there, Mr Malcolm?"

A Third Way

"Dad," Aaron whined, with an absurdly elongated "a", "Can I go on the computer?"

"No," Ryan said.

"Why?"

The "y" made the "a" seem terse.

"Because it is a waste of time."

"No it isn't."

"Yes it is. Do you think Marcus Rashford spends all of his life playing computer games?"

Aaron trudged away, grumbling about how Marcus Rashford probably didn't spend his life cleaning his room and doing geography homework. Ryan smiled, shook his head and opened a bottle of wine before taking a glass to Afia.

It was a rare night off for Ryan. He thought it was inappropriate for MPs to complain about their workload when soldiers, doctors and firefighters faced more difficult conditions. Still, if he looked at his calendar and found no debates, committee meetings, surgeries, charity functions or cocktail parties he could not help smiling.

Ryan was about to pour a glass of wine for himself when he heard the doorbell ring. Who could it be at 8:00 at night?

"Have I forgotten someone?" Ryan asked his wife.

She shrugged.

Ryan walked to the hall and peered through the peephole with very slight anxiety. He liked to think that he could welcome anyone and everyone. Still, after the killings of Jo Cox and David Amess, Ryan was not alone in feeling just a little cautious about unannounced guests.

It was Noel. Even through the peephole, Ryan could see that his old boss looked more than simply tired. He was swaying gently and his mouth was hanging open.

Ryan opened the door.

"Noel."

"I'm sorry to bother you," Noel said, "I should have rung."

Ryan remembered the days when Noel would call him at three o'clock in the morning and be outraged if he answered after more than five seconds. A surprise visit on a Wednesday evening was courteous by comparison. But he could not ignore the faint smell of alcohol.

"Yes, I've been drinking," said Noel, "Can I come in?"

"Of course."

Noel stumbled into the house. He looked, in his late middle age, like a bedraggled hawk. His cheeks had sunk, which made his pointed nose more prominent. His gaze was fierce and still.

"Do you want – *another* drink?"

"Scotch."

Noel led Ryan into the living room, where Afia was sitting, reading a book. He spread his arms.

"Afia! How are you even more beautiful than the last time we met?"

"Natural talent," Afia smiled, raising her eyebrows at Ryan when Noel turned around.

Aaron pottered into the room and stopped when he saw Noel.

"Who's this little man! I haven't seen you since you were a baby."

Noel leaned down in front of Aaron.

"You're keeping an eye on your daddy, aren't you? I used to be his boss, you know. You have to watch him at all times or he might get into trouble."

"*Really?*" Aaron asked.

"Was there something you wanted to talk about Noel?"

"Yes," said Noel, rising again, "Yes, actually. *Sorry* Afia but there is something political I want to talk to Ryan about."

"No problem with me," Afia said, looking rather less than devastated.

Ryan led Noel to the kitchen, to pour a neat Scotch, and then up to his office. He called it an "office" with his tongue planted in his cheek. It was only marginally bigger than an airing cupboard. But it gave him somewhere to work, read and think without the risk of Aaron's football screeching past his nose or into his face. Now he had a Kindle he did not need to fill it up with books, even if part of him felt like he had adopted the role of Quisling in the fall of civilisation.

Noel stood next to the window, brooding, while Ryan cleared papers off the chair. He looked like a general surveying the ruins of his army, though he was in fact surveying Ryan's long-neglected garden.

"What's up then, Noel?"

"What's up? What's up? What *isn't* up?"

For as long as Ryan had known him, Noel Griffiths had been a passionate man. Indeed, he had been a passionate man long before that. At Cambridge, or so legend had it, his response to Labour defeat in 1983 had been to punch a member of the Militant Tendency in the face. As an MP, when a much younger Ryan had been making him coffee, he had been one of Prime Minister Tony Blair's fiercest bulldogs.

Now, though, something had changed.

"This fucking government," spat Noel, "What can we do about it?"

"What do you mean?"

"What do I mean!? COVID cases? Rising! Corruption? Rampant! Brexit? Happened! It's too much, Ryan. Something has to give."

This was what Ryan had feared. Following his old mentor's Twitter posts, in which Noel raged against Brexit and the Tories, Ryan had noticed a descent from the imperiousness of a Roman senator to the outrage of a pub drunk. He was forever trying to rally his troops, not realising, it appeared, that most of them were 60-year-old geography teachers.

"You didn't even vote for us," Ryan smiled.

"Hm? Well, Corbyn was a maniac. No fault of yours, of course, but he's as much to blame for all of this as fucking Johnson."

"So, what are you thinking?"

"Look..."

Noel glanced out of the window again, as if concerned that government spies were lurking in the shadows. He bent towards Ryan and spoke in a hiss.

"Starmer can't do this by himself. He doesn't have it. That passion. That charisma. He's not *Tony,* understand?"

"So?"

"If we could convince Ed and Caroline to get on board - maybe even Nicola - we could build a progressive alliance. A government of national unity."

"Nicola Sturgeon? National unity?"

"Right now she has the Tories and no independence," Noel scowled, "Wouldn't she prefer no Tories and – and, er – a progressive devolution of powers?"

"Who is going to lead this alliance?"

"I'm not sure," admitted Noel, "But perhaps we need an outsider. Someone that people *know* but don't associate with *the system*. A centrist Trump!"

"Who?"

"How about this..."

Noel leaned even closer and smiled.

"Gary Lineker!"

The silence coagulated. Noel studied Ryan's face, waiting for his reaction.

"It sounds far-fetched."

"Well, we have to do *something*," Noel barked, finishing his drink and wiping phlegm and whisky from his lips, "Brexit. Cuts. Corruption. They're destroying everything we built! Our whole legacy!"

"I don't like the Tories any more than you," said Ryan, "But we can't go back to 2005. For most of the country that means Iraq, ID cards and mass immigration."

"I can't believe I'm hearing this," said Noel, shaking his head, "What about all our successes? The Good Friday

Agreement. SureStart. Did the 2012 Olympics mean *nothing* to you?"

"Held under a Conservative government."

"Clement Attlee was Prime Minister when Japan surrendered," Noel fumed, "But Winston Churchill won the war!"

"Don't you think you're being a bit extreme?"

"Who are you with?" Noel asked, eyes bulging, "Ryan, look at your wife. Your kid. Do you think the Tories *like* that?"

"Do the Tories like my wife?"

"*What she represents!*"

"What do you want me to say?" Ryan asked, "We can keep talking about Brexit - be a party of permanent opposition - or we can try and make ourselves electable."

"This is useless. I see you're not interested."

"I'm interested in what *works*," said Ryan, "In what can be done."

"*In what can be done,*" sneered Noel, "You're not *doing* anything."

"I think it's time you left."

Noel deflated. He looked like a shadow of the man that Ryan had seen treating journalists like they were errant schoolboys who had kicked a ball over his fence. Then he puffed himself up, stuck out his jaw and glowered.

"I don't want to argue with you, Ryan," he said, "I like you. But these are not normal times. This is not a normal government. We're dealing with people who want you to believe – to *sincerely* believe – that a man with COVID drove for miles to see a castle to test his eyesight. If they can get people to believe that, what else can they get people to believe? That we have to sell the NHS? That we can't hold elections? That foreigners have to wear yellow stars? I'm not going to put up with it Ryan. I'm going to do something."

"You're going to get home safely," said Ryan, shepherding Noel from the room.

"You know, I've never liked his politics," Afia said, after Noel had left, "I don't like *him*. But I *do* respect being so committed to your beliefs."

"I'm not sure he has beliefs," said Ryan, "New Labour is just who he *is*. He's New Labour so he hates Brexit. It's like being a Rangers fan who hates the Pope."

*

The Palace of Westminster was an impressive place to work. It was just a shame, Ryan reflected as he strolled around Parliament Square, that it was falling apart. What politician wants to spend millions of pounds on his workplace when his voters see hospitals close and taxes climb? A guaranteed vote loser. Far more sensible to hope that your opponents are in power on the day that it collapses – and that you have retired.

Ryan peered up at the grand Gothic exterior of the palace, always so much more imposing than its inhabitants. He remembered that he had forgotten to call Noel to see if he had arrived home the night before. Remembering his old friend's anger, he called his wife instead.

"Hi Sarah. Noel popped in last night. Not sure if he said. I just wanted to check he got home."

"Yes, he did. He's up and gone now. Did you have a fight or something? He was very agitated."

"Well, you know how can get."

She laughed.

"Poor Noel. A man of action with nothing to do."

Ryan laughed and finished the call. He approached the police barricade, pulling out his pass.

"Morning, guys."

Suddenly, Ryan heard a commotion from Parliament Square. The officers who had smiled as he had approached were looking beyond him, faces contorted in shock.

Ryan spun around. A man was stood on Parliament Square. An EU flag was draped across one of his shoulders and a Union Jack was hanging from the other. Flames were shooting up his jacket.

It was Noel. His hawkish gaze was pinned on Westminster Palace as the flames reached his shoulders.

"Fuck!"

The police officers and various passers-by sprinted across Parliament Square towards Noel. Dazed, Ryan followed them.

A huge man in an Old Glory shirt was first to reach Noel, and he knocked him to the ground. In a mess of bodies, the men dragged him around the grass and pressed their jackets on the flames. Another police officer appeared with a fire extinguisher and sprayed Noel silly. Then there were cries and the filthy smell of burned cloth and barbequed flesh.

*

"Will he be alright?"

"Physically, yes."

Noel drank his beer.

"The paramedics say he can't have used a lot of lighter fluid.".

"So?"

"Well, that means he probably didn't want to kill himself. Say what you like about Noel Griffiths but if he has a job then he gets the job done. In his mind this must have been some sort of weird publicity stunt."

"Isn't burning yourself *always* a weird publicity stunt?"

"I guess."

"Of course, I'd rather sit in the road or something."

"I'd rather people let me do my job."

Ryan cracked up another beer, realising that it was the first time he would have had more than one since the election.

"Well, he certainly was committed," said Afia.

"He *should* be committed," Ryan frowned, "Why did he have to be so *silly*? Why can't people be more *sensible*?"

"What do people have to do to be sensible?"

"Not too much," said Ryan, looking through the window at the rooftops and the stars beyond them, "And not too little."

Landfill

I

Tommy walked into the room looking as if he had not taken his sunglasses off in the last twenty years. Dropping onto a sofa, he laid his guitar case down with the elaborate care of a new mother laying down her child. Then he lit a cigarette.

"'Ello Pete."

From the other side of the room, Peter Baker nodded at his old bandmate and sipped his coffee.

"How's it going Tom?"

"Fucking great!"

Tommy spat his answer out as if he was offended to be asked – as if his greatness should be *obvious*. He scratched his elbow and hiccupped with the eerie suggestion of an urge to puke. Then he took another drag from his cigarette.

"An' you?"

"Alright."

It was a dark "alright", labouring under implications of a nagging wife, bad-tempered children, financial problems, a bad back, a sick dog and a leaking garage roof. But he was alright. What else was he meant to say?

He was talking to his booze-addled old bandmate, not a therapist.

"Where's Adam?" Tommy asked.

"On his way."

Tommy looked startled, and then proud, and then offended not to be the last to arrive.

"What have you been doing with yourself?" Peter asked.

Tommy sighed, as if he was Bowie being asked in 1974 why he was wearing make-up. *Wasn't it obvious?*

"*Music* man. Been playing with Baz from The Cocks and Billy from The Bitter Walnuts. Should be putting an EP out on Turncoat Records soon."

Peter nodded. He had recognised none of those names.

"Fuck man, it's really good," Tommy enthused, coming alive, "Sort of dream pop meets punk in a techno club, know what I mean?"

Peter nodded. He did not.

"Wha' 'bout yourself?" asked Tommy, "Got some projects on the go?"

"I've got two kids," said Peter, "And I work in tech support."

Peter could see Tommy's eyes glaze over even through his dark sunglasses.

"Nice."

The door swung open and Adam walked in with the bearing of a man looking for the exit.

"Sorry," he said, by way of introduction, "Car trouble."

Once, The Long Dark Nights were going to be the next big thing. Their single "As You Like It" spread across MySpace like a virus through a packed departure lounge. After a swaggering performance on Popworld it reached number 3 in the charts. The next year, their debut album *Causes of Crime* was described by *NME* as having "the charm of The Libertines, the swagger of Oasis and the knowing intelligence on Franz Ferdinand." At the launch party, Peter drank a bottle of champagne without taking a breath. He had gone from playing to six people in an Essex pub to playing for thousands of fans in the Astoria. He had gone from blue-tacking Buzzcocks posters to his bedroom wall to drinking beers with Pete Shelley. Now came a life of riffs, and stadiums, and sex.

Then the album didn't sell. Well, it did. But it didn't. *Causes of Crime* limped up the charts, stalled in the thirties and then disappeared into the nothingness of the triple figures. Perhaps the band had an image problem, label bosses wondered. Too hipster. Not hipster enough. Perhaps they had had the wrong singles. Perhaps, just perhaps, the British public had had their fill of gangly white boys playing Gallagheresque indie pop.

Suddenly, journalists who had been knocking at their doors were nowhere to be found. PR reps who had been hanging around their gigs dematerialized. *NME* endorsements dried up like raindrops beneath the sun.

Peter worked furiously hard on the second album. He wanted every note to be in its right place. Adam spent a lot of time on the Internet and Tommy spent a lot of time drinking but Peter analysed every verse and chorus with almost scientific care. He called the album *When...* in a fond reference to his favourite Malcolm McDowell film.

It was futile. The media were determined to correct for their mistake and would have shat on the album if it had been a collaboration between Radiohead and Johannes Sebastian Bach. "So lazy, routine and unimaginative that it makes *EastEnders* look as if it were directed by Quentin Tarantino," was how *NME* put it in their 3/10 review, "If this is indie rock then pass the pop music."

Years afterwards, Peter found a novel written by the *NME* critic and left an Amazon review saying it was "the biggest pile of crap I've seen since I was on an elephant safari." The album sank like a brick.

The band were going through personal problems as well. Adam was reading about existentialism and saying "why" when Peter asked him to lay down a rhythm. Tommy, meanwhile, did not have a drinking problem as much as a drinking catastrophe. For breakfast, he washed down vodka with a cold Guinness, and his idea of a healthy lunch was Jack Daniels with *Diet* Coke and not the real thing. If he played a song in the right key it was a nice surprise and if he also tuned his guitar it was a miracle.

At one gig, Peter found some passing satisfaction as he watched young, cheerful faces sing along with him. Then he saw them reel away in horror and disgust as a sickly yellow liquid splattered over them. He turned around and saw Tommy gurning half-consciously, with his wilted member dribbling piss.

The band fell apart. Adam went back to Essex to live with his parents and watch *Loose Change* and *Zeitgeist* on a loop. Tommy played with more bands than he ate solid meals. Peter flirted with the concept of a solo career but it spluttered out. Later he would say that his heart had not been in it but the truth was that the fans had not been into it. Soon, he was back to playing for six people in an Essex pub.

Looking back, Peter wished that he had had more sense. So many bands had been the future of music between 2003 and 2007 and he had forgotten half of them by the turn of the decade. Most of them could be summarised as "The Noun". The Rakes. The Others. The Horrors. The Twang. The Wombats. The Pigeon Detectives. The Kooks. The Maccabees. The Enemy. The Automatic. The British music industry, and the British media, were hoping, hungering, to recapture the excitement and the energy of Britpop and were throwing any collection of pale, vaguely tuneful young men at the wall of the public consciousness to see if they would stick. Most of them slid off. It was only natural. The Long Dark Nights were no exception.

"Jesus," Adam said, fiddling with his drumsticks as if unsure of whether to hold them with his fingers or his feet. Tommy plugged in his guitar and rattled off a few loud, irrelevant chords. Peter asked himself, with measured panic, if he still remembered the words to his own songs.

They were practicing in a converted warehouse. Years before, Peter would have attached some kind of romantic allegory to this. *It was an industrial revolution for indie rock! Harnessing the creative energy of the modern world! Futurism!* Now he just thought it was fitting for what was, when it came down to it, another job.

"The boys are back together," said Tommy, grinning broadly, " 'S'like those gangster films. Y'know, we're gettin' back together for one last heist."

"We're not doing anything criminal," said Peter, humourlessly, wondering if it would be more dignified if they were.

"What are we trying first," asked Tommy, ""As You Like It"? I could play that in my sleep. I could play it *dead*."

Peter *one, two, three*-d into the microphone and picked up his bass. He plucked a few notes from "Come As You Are" and wondered if he should graduate to "Seven Nation Army" to complete his metamorphosis into a thirteen-year-old boy setting out on his long and winding road to pussy.

Tommy launched himself into the riff, like nothing had changed since 2005. Peter felt anticipation rising from his gut to his throat as he waited for his moment.

"I came here t---"

There was a thud as Adam totally misjudged the rhythm and hammered the snare drum. He cursed and wiped his forehead. Peter stopped and scratched his nose. Tommy carried on thrashing away at his guitar, transcending the riff and cartwheeling into a preposterous solo.

"And again..."

Tommy barrelled back into his intro and Adam whirled away at the drums. Peter cleared his throat and clutched the microphone.

"I came here to sa---"

A drumstick slipped from Adam's hand. He hurled the other onto the floor and snarled. Peter took a gulp of water as if singing eight words had dried out his throat.

Adam blundered from the room, in search of a toilet, or an escape route. Peter let him go. In the past they might have argued about it but they were too old. Peter was not sure if this could be explained by maturation or fatigue.

Tommy grinned across the room at Peter.

"You're looking bigger, pal," he said.

Peter looked down at his front. It was true. He had gained a couple of pounds. Fifteen years before, he and Tommy had been razor thin – all angles, like a physical manifestation of pop punk. Tommy was still slim, if strained, like a dying flower. Peter's stomach, though, was peering over his belt, and his arms and legs were full from gardening and lasagne.

"True," he said, "I could kick your ass."

Tommy cackled.

"Did you ever think we would be playing together again?" he asked.

"Not in Saudi Arabia."

"True."

Peter had been sitting in his shed smoking a cigarette when his phone had rung.

"Hello?"

He was looking out across his pride and joy: a little patch of grass, surrounded by clumps of soggy flowers.

Well, his children were his pride and joy. But his garden was quiet.

"Mr Baker?"

"Yes?"

"My name is Mahmud and I am a representative of Prince Mahir bin Abdulaziz, Deputy Minister of Interior in the Kingdom of Saudi Arabia."

"Well, I'm Peter Baker, representative of Peter Baker."

"Ha ha ha," said the man in a smooth impersonation of a laugh, "Very funny, Mr Baker. Well, are you the same Peter Baker who was the lead singer of the band "The Long Dark Nights"?"

"Yes," said Peter, wondering which of his friends was playing a prank on him.

"Prince Mahir has instructed me to invite your band to play a concert in Riyadh in our country," said Mahmud in greasy tones, speaking as if he was conducting an aural massage, "It would be an honour to welcome you."

"Our band has not existed for more than a decade."

"That might be so," crooned Mahmud, "But Prince Mahir's son is an admirer of your song "As You Like It" and your album *Causes of Crime*. He would like you to perform at his seventeenth birthday party. Of course, we can offer generous compensation."

Peter looked across his little garden at his little garage, with its leaking roof. It was not a bad house, really. It was big enough, and in a safe neighbourhood. But if you had expected steak you would not be as happy with a chicken sandwich as a man who had expected a pot noodle.

"Don't you guys cut people's hands off?"

There was a pause. The silence was abrasive.

"Would you like some time to think about it, Mr Baker?"

Peter thought about it.

"Sure."

His cigarette had gone out. He walked back into his house. Thumbing "Mahmud Ahmed Abdulaziz" into Google he found a reference to the spokesman in a *Gulf News* article about oil contracts. His statement sounded like his conversation.

Lila was in the kitchen peeling potatoes.

"Jenny's shoes are broken," she said.

"Oh?"

"Her feet are getting wet."

"I'll take her out to buy some more."

He thought, to his private shame, about the *drip drip drip* of expenses leaking into their lives. He opened the fridge, pulled out a slice of yellow cheese and ate it in one.

"I'm making lunch," said Lila, without looking at him.

"Sorry."

He wrapped his arms around his chest and rubbed his biceps.

"Cold in here."

He tapped the boiler. *Tap tap tap.*

"There's something wrong with it," said Lila.

"There's something wrong with the weather," said Peter, "It's *April*."

"It's *England*," said Lila, still not glancing up.

Drip drip drip.

As he lay in bed that night, feeling no more close to sleep than to Australia, Peter thought about ringing some music journalist to tell them that he had turned down a gig in Saudi Arabia. It would make for a nice story. A few people would say kind things about his integrity. Others would claim he was making it up.

Then it would disappear. No one would listen to his music. They would go back to Beyonce, who had sung for the Gaddafis, or Jennifer Lopez, who had sung happy birthday to the delectably named Turkmen dictator Gurbanguly Berdymukhamedov. Principles were for people who died penniless.

"Frankly," said a nasal voice in his ear, which had haunted him so many times, "Listening to the dregs of landfill indie in 2021 is not something we would wish even on Mohammed bin Salman. Sending the Long Dark Nights to Saudi Arabia might have been considered something close to an act of war."

The next morning Peter went into his garden, in a soupy drizzle, and called Mahmud. Oil leaked from his mobile phone as the spokesman answered.

"Mr Baker, so glad to hear from you."

"How *much* compensation?"

"How much would you like?"

Numbers whirled in Peter's mind.

"Fifty thousand each, plus expenses."

"Certainly."

Peter wondered if he should have said a hundred thousand pounds, and if it was too late to correct himself.

"I have to ask the other guys," he said.

"Of course."

"You know, if it was sixty thousand it might be easier to persuade them."

Tommy needed no persuading. Between noisy drags on a cigarette, morbidly amplified by his mobile phone, he enthused about the power of *the music man.*

"Saudi Arabia sounds like a shit place," he drawled, "No booze. No fags. The woman wear..."

His mind flailed around for an acceptable term.

"...those things. But maybe music can touch their hearts, you know. Make them see life differently. Besides, I miss playing with you motherfuckers."

"One more thing, Tommy. I hate to ask this bu---"

"I'm sober, yeah."

Adam was more difficult to persuade. He was difficult to *find*. He didn't have the same number. He wasn't on Facebook, Instagram, Twitter or LinkedIn. His family had moved out of their old house. Was he in England? Was he alive?

Eventually, Peter found a mutual friend who told him that Adam could only be contacted on a mysterious app called Telegram. It took Peter a long time to work out how to use the damn thing and when he finally managed to send Adam a note he heard nothing back for a day. He was thinking about hiring a session musician when his phone rang.

"I haven't played the drums for years," Adam sighed.

"I haven't sung," said Peter, "Well, unless you count the shower."

"Why do they want *us*?"

"The kid is a fan. He probably heard us on a video game."

"It's all so weird," said Adam, quietly, "*Too* weird."

"Well, perhaps there is a deep international conspiracy built around a long forgotten indie band. What do you think?"

"I don't like it."

"Adam," Peter said, gritting his teeth, "It's for sixty thousand."

There was a long, meditative pause.

"Sixty thousand *pounds*?"

"Yeah."

Adam sighed.

"Well, I suppose it's meant to be."

As the three men practiced, they slowly found their groove. Adam had always sweated as he drummed. Now, sweat was pouring down his face like a mountain stream. It pooled in his lap and sank into his trousers, leaving a dark patch.

Tommy's features twisted and writhed as he played. He panted pornographically as his fingers danced around the strings. Peter, though, was feeling self-conscious. He was singing, sure, in time and in tune, but he could sense that he was standing like a mannequin, and when he tried to move it was with the herky-jerky motions of a marionette. Perhaps it was all in his head, he told himself. Perhaps it made him look like Ian Curtis.

He closed his eyes and imagined that there was a mob of screaming fans in front of him. He closed his eyes and imagined that he was in the Electric Ballroom, fifteen years before, and 2000 wild, hungry eyes were watching him, and 1000 wild, hungry mouths were singing along with him. His doubts faded for as long as he forgot about them.

They took a break. Peter walked across the room to collect his little pack of damp cheese and tomato sandwiches. As he took a bite, he heard the *click* of a can opening behind him. He spun around and saw Tommy sipping an energy drink.

"What?"

"Those things are bad for you."

"So?"

Tommy glugged the rest of his drink.

"Do we 'ave to quarantine in Saudi?"

"I don't think so," Peter shrugged.

"I bet we 'ave to wear those fucking masks."

"For sixty thousand pounds I'll wear a gimp suit as well."

"Hey Adam," Tommy shouted, to where Adam was slouched in the corner, "You always knew wha' was up. What do you think about these *fucking* masks?"

"Oh, I dunno..."

94

Adam rolled a drumstick between his fingers. His brow furrowed and his blonde hair bristled.

"Well," he said, his irises darkening, "I mean, first you have to think about where the virus came from. There was a lab in Wuhan that was studying coronaviruses. You want to tell me that that was a coincidence?"

He dug his drumsticks into the flesh beneath his chin and his eyes darted around.

"Then our government does *nothing, until* the virus is in Britain, and they shut down *everything – just* like they did in China. You can't even go for a walk without being harassed – and Britain has no fewer deaths than Sweden, *where everything stays open*! So, you have to ask yourself who knew about COVID, and when, and you have to ask yourself why governments were so desperate to seize power for themselves. How can we trust them next time, you know, and how can we *stop* them?"

Adam stopped, sniffed and tapped the snare drum pointlessly.

"We have to ask questions," he shrugged, "That's all I'm saying."

"I'm too old to ask questions," Peter said, "My kids ask *me* questions. Once you're 30, 35, 40, you have to know the answers or pretend to know them."

"Here's how I look at it," said Tommy, raising his finger philosophically, "Fuck COVID *and* fuck politicians."

He sat back, folding his arms, as if he had answered the question of why there was something rather than nothing.

Peter went for a piss. As he washed his hands, he looked in the mirror and tried to reproduce the wild-eyed, stiff-jawed face that he had used onstage. It was a manic, furious expression that made people wonder what the hell was going through his mind. The answer, typically, was nothing.

He jutted out his chin but his jowls still sagged.

Adam walked into the toilet and splashed water on his face.

"What happened to you?" asked Peter, "Getting hold of you was like looking for Lord Lucan."

"Nothing. I keep to myself."

"What have you been doing?"

Adam shrugged.

"Well, I made some money on crypto. Then I lost it."

"Gambling? Drugs?"

"No, I really lost it," Adam sniffed, "I forgot the password."

Back in the rehearsal space, they ran through "Coda". It had been the last song on their first album. It had been meant to be their "epic", though Peter reflected that it had been "epic" inasmuch as it had been six minutes long. Still, it was a good tune. Peter sang, Tommy stabbed the strings and Adam built the rhythm up from a steady patter to a furious beat. Somehow, through the song, the three of them became a seamless whole, operating on pure muscle memory.

"*Tha's* what I'm talkin' about," snapped Tommy as they finished.

Peter nodded and smiled.

He drove home through Braintree. *Braintree*. The name had always fascinated him. It combined the wonders of human intelligence with the wonders of the natural world and yet had the same dismal connotations as "Slough" and "Leamington Spa".

A lot of their first album had been about living there. A lot of the second had been about living in London. That was the tradition. You wrote one album about trying to escape your hometown and the next about how it had been a big disappointment.

He drove past the school where he had first met Tommy and Adam – then, respectively, a hyperactive prankster who would take his dad's acoustic guitar to football practice and a quiet, cheerful boy who drummed his fingers on his desk. He drove past the pub where they had played their first gig. It was a cream-coloured bastion of pool-mad functional alcoholism where the power had been cut after two songs.

Wasn't it amazing that this little band from Braintree had made it to number 3 in the charts? Well, perhaps the word "amazing" should be reserved for Jesus returning from the dead or Stalin going from being a Georgian seminarian to the General Secretary of the Communist Party of the Soviet Union. But it was still impressive.

Peter parked his car, which grunted and groaned as it stopped, and walked into the house. Abigail ran past, on some obscure secret mission, and collided with his leg. He scooped his daughter up, chuckling her startled cries away, and went into the living room. Lila was sweeping the powdered remains of biscuits from the floor.

"Where's Richard?" Peter asked.

"In his room," Lila said, "He's sulking because he wants to go to Saudi Arabia with you."

"Definitely not," said Peter, thinking about his war-mad eight-year-old, "He'd end up in Syria."

"That one is going to be devastated," said Lila, nodding at their daughter, who was falling asleep on her daddy's chest.

"Life."

"How was the practice?"

"Not bad."

"You don't sound very excited."

"Well, it's hardly Glastonbury."

Lila snorted, stood and tied her long brown hair up in a ponytail.

"*My* work was fine, thank you," she said.

"Sorry. I mean --- good."

Peter looked at his wife. Specifically, he looked at her ass. How could he not? The first thing that he had noticed had been her ass, fifteen years before, swaying hypnotically as she had served up cocktails in a Shoreditch bar. The second thing that he had noticed, somewhat to his own surprise, had been her self-assurance. He had got used, in a matter of months, to girls wanting to talk to him but he had known that there was something special about Lila when he had realised how much he wanted to talk to her.

Still, for the first months of their relationship he had carried the quiet suspicion that she had got lucky. He was a rock star and she was a barmaid. Since then, that suspicion had shrivelled up and mutated into its opposite.

Carrying his daughter up the stairs to bed, Peter snuck a glance into Richard's room. The light was off and he could hear heavy breathing. He tucked Abigail in and went down to his wife, who was curled up on the sofa, reading.

"Hungry?"

He leaned over her and kissed her on the lips.

"Hungry for you."

She kissed back, then held his chin and pushed him back.

"I know you meant that to sound sexy but it *didn't.*"

Peter snorted, trying to seem sarcastic but sounding more mammalian. He jumped onto the sofa and planted one hand on her side and one hand on her ass. She laughed and clutched his shirt.

There was a crash. Peter and Lila looked at each other and then fell off the sofa in a muddle of limbs before running up the stairs to the children's rooms. Richard was sitting up in bed, looking confused, with his headphones in his ears and his phone in his hand. Peter and Lila ran to Abigail's room and found her standing in the dark, surrounded by pieces of glass, the sharp edges of which leered up at her like crocodile teeth. Peter guessed that she had been trying to make the door when she had knocked a little ornament off her shelf.

"My mermaid," Abigail sniffed, as if she had just understood the concept of death.

II

"Are we doing the right thing?" asked Adam.

"What do you mean?"

"Going to Saudi Arabia," the drummer said, driving the tips his drumsticks into his legs, "You know, they're killing kids in Yemen."

"Sure," said Peter, "I don't like that any more than you do. But look at it like this, you pay taxes, right?"

"Sometimes."

"And Britain sells arms to the Saudis?"

"Yes."

"So, what is worse, *taking* money from the people killing kids in Yemen or *giving* it to them?"

Adam thought about what Peter was saying.

"You mean I shouldn't pay my taxes?"

"I mean that life is complicated and as long as you aren't hurting anyone you shouldn't think about it too much."

Tommy ambled in, twenty minutes late. Peter pointedly looked at his watch and Tommy held up his hand. Bandages stretched around his palm, beneath his fingers. Blood had soaked through and formed a dark red blotch.

"What *happened*?"

"Fuckin' glass exploded in me 'and," the guitarist slurred, "But I was lucky. The doctor said that if the glass 'ad gone anuvva way it could 'ave taken off me fingers."

"Jesus," Peter said, thinking about how close their Saudi trip had come to disaster, "How does it feel?"

"Well," said Tommy, thoughtfully, "It's going to 'urt like fuck tomorrer but right now I'm on so many painkillers I'm *flyin'*."

"What was in the glass?"

"Eh?"

"What was in the glass?"

"Dunno. Orange juice I think."

They rehearsed. Peter was relieved that Tommy's playing seemed unaffected. His face twitched and his mouth hung open, but it always had done. As they rattled seamlessly through their songs, he was more concerned about his bandmates's mental than physical condition.

On the morning of their flight, Peter arrived early at the airport and smoked a cigarette as he watched galaxies of travellers arrive. Some were holidaying. Some were going on business trips. It struck him, too late, that he should have demanded first class tickets. He smoked another cigarette.

A text arrived: "where r u cunt im here already". Peter found Tommy in the terminal, looking refreshed and sipping from a bottle of orange juice. He did his best not to look surprised.

"Thought you woulda got here earlier," said Tommy.

"Well, it was hard saying goodbye to the kids."

"Oh yeah," said Tommy, frowning, "I 'ad a terrible time saying bye to Jimi."

"Jimi?"

"My cat."

They waited for Adam. Tommy finished his orange juice and bought another. Peter drank a coke and scanned his phone. He had thought about emailing a couple of journalists to tell them that the Long Dark Nights were getting back together. Then again, perhaps it was better if it remained their little secret.

Minutes crept by. A disembodied woman's voice announced flight after flight. Peter checked his phone more regularly, as if the very act would inspire it to ring. He tried to call Adam but his phone was off.

"Where *is* he?" Peter asked.

"If he *doesn't* come," said Tommy, thoughtfully, "Perhaps we can find a drummer in Saudi Arabia."

"I don't think Saudi Arabia is full of musicians," Peter said.

"What d'ya mean musicians? I'm talking about a drummer."

103

Time slunk on. Peter tried to call Adam again, to no avail. He and Tommy went outside for so many cigarettes he felt as if a rat had made its home in his throat. As the departure time approached, he wondered if they *should* head through security without the drummer. Then Adam appeared, shouldering his bag like a teenage boy slouching reluctantly into school.

"Missed the train," he said.

"Why was your phone off?"

"I keep it off unless I really need it."

"But how do you *know* you---"

Peter breathed through his nose. There was no point in arguing about it. Besides, they had no time.

Inevitably, the plane was delayed. Peter, Tommy and Adam sat in the departure lounge. Britain might have opened up but tension remained. People stole suspicious glances at one another for sitting too close and not wearing masks, or for appearing aggravated that they were sitting too close or not wearing masks. The atmosphere was as thick as school canteen stew. A kind of bored hostility reigned.

"Amazing, innit," said Tommy, meditatively, "Somewhere so different from ours. People so different from us. But they still love our music. They still love our songs. Tha's power, man. *Soft* power."

"We're playing at a kid's birthday party," Peter grunted, "What kind of power is that?"

Tommy smiled and shrugged.

"*Soft* power."

Peter took a sip from a bottle of lukewarm Coke. The airport bars looked tempting. He would have loved to drink a few beers before the plane took off to Riyadh. But he did not want Tommy to get drunk and make a scene when they got there, and, if he was honest, he did not want to do the same himself.

He checked his phone. Lila had not rung or called. He guessed that it was time to ring. His wife picked up just before he was sent to voicemail.

"Hey."

"We're just waiting for our flight."

"Okay," she said, "Call me when you can."

"I'm calling you now."

There was a chilly pause.

"I'm getting dinner for the kids."

"How are they doing?"

"Fine."

"Why are you sounding pissy with me?" Peter grumbled, "I'm sorry I'm going, if that's what you're mad about, but I'm not going for a party, it's a job."

105

"Yeah, I know."

"I don't get you," Peter said, flaring up as he heard the spark in her voice, "I hardly ever leave. You're acting like I'm always out on tour."

"You *are* always out on tour," Lila said, bluntly, "A tour of your own head. You've been doing the circuit there since 2009."

"Don't be silly," Peter said, without much conviction.

"Get it out of your system," she said, "Then come home."

Peter put the phone down and walked back to Tommy and Adam, pulling an exaggerated *women!* face that no one noticed. Tommy was frowning intensely, looking at the ground, and Peter forgot his phone call as he wondered what was wrong.

"Alright?"

"Alright," Tommy muttered, his accent receding as he twitched with rage, "Just – no smoking area? It's inhuman. It's *obscene.*"

In the plane, Peter focused on his breathing as the aircraft grumbled down the runway, giving every sign that it was about to explode in a shower of twisted metal and broken limbs.

He caught and laughed at himself. Imagine if he *had* been successful. He would have been flying all the time!

How would he have dealt with *that*? Really, it was good how things had turned out. Really good.

Once the plane was in the air, Peter relaxed. He put on his headphones and listened to some music. Talking Heads and Sonic Youth burbled in his ears until the tracklist took a left turn and burst into "Apply Some Pressure" by Maximo Park. Glowing with nostalgia, he turned to "Hounds of Love" by The Futureheads and "Retreat" by The Rakes. What had it all meant? Not much. It had meant being young. It was better than being old.

"America" by Razorlight appeared on the playlist and Peter fell asleep.

When he woke up, the plane was about to land. It felt like waking up not from but *to* a nightmare. He gripped the armrest as the plane juddered, feeling his stomach shake like a boat in a storm. Tommy had inexplicably turned a paler shade of pale.

"Fuck me," he mumbled, "I don't think I've ever done this sober."

Peter looked out of the window. Before him was mile upon mile of sand, an immense arid wilderness. Britain, with its little fields, and trees, and hedgerows, gave one a sense of order and fertility in nature, but here was stark existential fact.

A city appeared and gradually densified. Buildings studded the desert, clinging onto the sand like barnacles onto stone. Peter wondered how people had ever built their lives there. It felt difficult enough in Braintree.

Finally, the plane skidded down the runway and muttered to a halt. Peter, Tommy and Adam eased themselves out of their seats and stumbled into the open air. Saudi sun slapped them round the face. It was twice as hot as it had been in England and so dry that Peter felt like a plum shrivelling up into a prune.

They walked across the tarmac, in a crowd of Arabs in long, elegant robes and English businessmen sweating in their ill-chosen suits. Going through customs was perhaps more intimidating than the plane ride itself. The border guard surveyed Peter's e-visa with a studious contempt. Peter wondered if he had inspired special disdain by being a musician or if this was how the man treated everyone. Finally, he was nodded out into arrivals.

Everything in King Khalid Airport was clean to the point of being antiseptic. Peter and Tommy waited to collect their guitars. They had not bothered to bring more equipment. It would have been a waste of money, and, besides, Adam did not have his own drums.

In the departure lounge, a man in robes was flanked by hulking bodyguards. Peter walked cautiously towards him.

"Peter?"

A voice like honey.

"Mahmud."

"Pleasure to meet you. This way. I'll take you to your hotel."

They drove to the hotel in the sort of sleek black car people probably enter without leaving alive. The bodyguards sat behind them, unacknowledged but impossible to ignore, with swollen frames and sunglasses.

"You must be tired," said Mahmud, displaying his impressive Anglophile credentials in his assumption that any amount of travel exhausts a man, "You have today and tomorrow to rest and relax before the concert."

Peter looked out at the street, where glass towers stood in splendid anonymity.

The hotel was shaped for vice, yet excluded vice. It was plush and featureless, lavish and forgettable. It was sort of place developers throw up in other capitals so bankers can get trashed and shag expensive escorts. But there was no alcohol and most of the women were veiled.

Peter sat in the lobby and sipped orange juice. There was something sexy about women in headdresses. The veils made their eyes brighter somehow. He told himself he was probably being orientalist – *exoticising* them. But he had felt the same peculiar hint of excitement when women had worn face masks during the pandemic. The unseen added potential, while emphasising everything else.

At least the social conservatism of Saudi Arabia meant there would be fewer temptations. Or fewer opportunities. Peter scratched his lip. He had betrayed his wife on three occasions in the noughties. The first time, with a leggy blonde in Bristol, he had told himself it was okay because she had only jerked him off. The second time, with an Irish redhead in Liverpool, he had told himself it was okay because she had only *sucked* him off. The third time he had got drunk and banged a cute brunette in his hotel room in Berlin. He had told himself it was okay because it was only once. But he knew that the compulsion to rationalise the act to himself made him guiltier than if he had simply not cared. He had never done so much as kissed a fan again, though fewer and fewer had shown any interest in being kissed.

Tommy shambled in, from where he had smoking in the street, looking hot and irritable.

"I'm boilin'," he said.

"Why don't you take your jacket off?"

"Are kiddin' me? It's freezin' in 'ere."

"So, take your jacket off when you're outside."

"What is this? The fucking army?"

Tommy sat back.

"God it's boring here. I thought England was boring. This place makes Braintree look like Las Vegas. Hey..."

He looked at Peter.

110

"If this gig goes well, what about playing in England again? I 'ear from people all the time who want us to get back together."

"All the time?"

"It's 'appened."

"I don't know," said Peter, "You can't bring back the past. I wish you could, but there's nothing sadder than old men's delusions."

"Old?" Tommy sniffed, "Speak fer yerself."

"Gentlemen," said Mahmud, appearing like a genie, "Would you like to see your venue?"

They agreed. Peter was not sure what he was expecting. A sideroom in one of the more obscure palaces, perhaps. He knew Saudi Arabia was as Islamic a nation as Islamic nations got and Muslims were not famously keen on popular music or, indeed, music in general beyond the call to prayer. It was not surprising if the spawn of royalty indulged themselves, as hypocrisy is a blessing of privilege, but he did not think that they would want to make a show of it.

He was stunned when they pulled up outside a stadium. It was not Wembley, perhaps, but *it was a stadium*. A giant stage was being erected in the middle of the pitch by dozens of men, moving with the controlled efficiency of ants.

"I thought this was *a birthday party*," Peter said, marvelling, "You could fit thousands in here."

"We will," said Mahmud, smoothly, "It is a party in honour of Prince Mahir's son."

"I thought you guys were against this sort of thing," said Peter.

"Against music? Mr Baker, we had BTS in 2019. Didn't you know?"

Peter wondered if that was some sort of epidemic.

"Prince Mohammed bin Salman is carrying us forward into the next era of Saudi life," marvelled Mahmud, "We must maintain our Islamic principles, of course, but we must also be open to the world. So, we have had wrestling. We have had pop stars. Now we have you, one of the most famous rock bands in the world."

Peter bit his tongue.

The next day crawled by. He drank so many coffees that his blood must have been the same colour as Saudi petroleum. Tommy twitched his way through breakfast and then disappeared to his room. Adam sat peacefully and read a book.

"You're looking very calm," said Peter.

"I've spent years waiting for something crazy to happen," Adam shrugged, "And this is pretty crazy."

They drove to the stadium in the early afternoon and had a quick rehearsal. Every song sounded crap. They should have been playing in a pub, not a stadium. Peter calmed himself with the thought that a Saudi audience would have as much experience of rock music as he had of nuclear physics. *Anything* might sound impressive.

The stadium was filling up with people. Young, lean Saudi men and girls in their hijabs were taking seats. They had not had so many people watching them since Reading 2006, and that had been a major disappointment because the crowd had been waiting for Dizzee Rascal and had shown all the enthusiasm of 15-year-olds in a school assembly.

Peter walked around the stage, fiddling with the kit. Everything had to be right. The guitars were tuned. The drums were in position. The microphones were working. Bottles of sparkling water sat around the stage.

Everything was ready.

"Where is Tommy?" Adam asked.

Peter looked around.

"Fuck!"

The guitarist was nowhere to be seen. Peter snatched his phone out of his pocket and tried to call him, hearing *beep beep beep.* Where was the prick? He had no desire to sent out a search party. He suspected that when the police went out looking for someone they did not always return.

"Where did you see him last?"

"He was talking to some guys."

"Why did you let him *do* that?" Peter said, exasperated, "You can't let him talk to guys. You can't let him talk to girls. You can't let him talk to *anyone*. He gets ideas."

Peter wondered how the hell he was going to explain to a bunch of cold-blooded Saudi Arabian officials that his dumb guitarist had ruined the prince's party. At that moment, Tommy sidled up, chewing gum.

"Yo."

"Where the *fuck* have you been?"

"I got lost."

He was swaying faintly. Peter smelled a hint of vodka.

"You've been drinking."

"'Aven't."

"Yes, you have."

"Oh, alright, I 'ave."

Tommy sniffed, looking, in his leather jacket, like a defiant schoolboy in a ratty blazer.

"But you 'ave to take yer opportunities man. Drinking is easy at 'ome. It's nothing special. Getting pissed in Saudi Arabia is different. It's a challenge. It's a story. It's something I'm gonna remember for the rest of my..."

"Alright," sighed Peter, "Where did you get the booze? No, don't tell me that. Just eat more gum and *concentrate*."

He could hear the rumbling of the crowd. Some kind of Saudi MC made an announcement that Peter inferred from its hushed, awed tone was in honour of the prince. There was a polite round of applause. Then came a strangled announcement of "De Long Dark Nights" and a stagehand waved them out through the curtains.

As soon as he picked his bass up and heard the growl of Tommy's guitar behind him, all of Peter's doubts and fears disintegrated. It was 2005 again. He felt ageless and uprooted. He was not old. He was not in Saudi Arabia. He was in some sort of transcendent performing space, amid the snarling riffs and thunderous percussion.

The crowd shifted before him. Waves of upstretched arms bore smartphones aloft, twinkling like moonlight on an open sea. As Peter bellowed the opening lines of "As You Like It" he could have sworn that he heard the Saudis singing along with him. Did they know the words? Did they know the song? Where had his Saudi royalties been all of these years?

Who cared. Tommy's playing was perfect. Adam's rhythms were on point. As he saw his guitarist grinning across the stage, Peter remembered why such different people had ever been friends. It was not because they had had hours of enlightening conversation. It was not because they had loved cooking, or hiking, or playing football together. It was for *moments like these*. It was for moments that made everything else worth living through.

Lila had been right. He had been lying to her and to himself when he had claimed that he was only doing it as a job. He had missed the intensity of experience.

The band swaggered into their hotel after the gig, cackling. They took the lift up to their floor.

"Hey," said Peter, frowning at Tommy, who had his guitar case on his arm and an amp case in his hand, "You didn't come here with an amp. Why did you take it?"

"Come in," Tommy said, nodding towards his hotel room.

Peter and Adam followed the guitarist inside, where he put down the amp case, unzipped it and extracted two glistening bottles of vodka.

"You *cunt*," Peter marvelled.

"Look," said Tommy, "What *are* we? A rock band or a choir? We just 'ad a fuckin' *banger* of a concert. Are you tellin' me we're going ter drink coffee an' orange juice?"

"Okay," said Peter, "*Okay*. Pour me a drink."

They drank. They laughed. They talked about the bizarreness of it all. They reminisced, remembering the early days of being packed into an old people carrier like anchovies into a can, and those brief, glorious times

116

when they could sign so many chests of beautiful young women that their wrists seized up and ached.

Adam retired to bed.

"How are people going to remember us?" asked Tommy, whose pronunciation mysteriously became more comprehensible the more he drank.

"They aren't."

"Eh?"

"Do you remember everyone you made out with in secondary school?"

Tommy thought about it.

"I don't remember everyone I made out with last year."

"Well, that's who we were. They won't remember us. But we mattered at the time."

"No," said Tommy, shaking his head, "That's not enough for me. I want to be remembered like I was their first fuck."

"You're more of an artist than I am," said Peter, downing one last shot, "I'm going to bed."

Peter stumbled out into the corridor. The silence in the hotel was unearthly. All he could hear was the hum of air conditioning.

He was drunk. *God*, he was drunk. He had not noticed when he had been drinking because the post-gig adrenaline had kept him afloat but now he could feel his brain being submerged in alcohol. Had he eaten? No. Had he drunk a lot of water? No. Was he old? Yes. It was a woeful combination.

Fuck. No one could find *him* like this. Tommy *always* acted as if he was half-cut but Peter would have no excuses. He realised, as he marched down the corridor, that he could not remember where his room was. Had he passed it? Was he walking in the wrong direction?

"Sauna" said a sign. Sauna? That was great! He could hide in there and sweat out all the alcohol. Peter lurched through a pair of doors and gasped in the cool freshness of the room that he had found.

This was not a sauna. It was a gym. Rows of weights lay on their racks like handguns in an armoury. Enormous machines rested like sleeping mutants in some sort of alien ship.

Peter saw himself in the mirror. Sweaty. Gurning. Overweight. He was the very definition of middle age. He picked up a weight. It was one of the lightest but he still felt a twinge run down his arm.

This was it – back to the mediocrity and regularity of life, all he deserved as a mediocre, regular man.

Looking in the mirror, Peter saw someone else: a pale, skinny-fat man in a flannel shirt and a pair of jeans tight enough to burst his testicles.

"The Long Dark Nights had their moment in the sun," the man sneered, in a familiar nasal voice, "But their songs did not inhabit darkness or light as much as dreary English grey."

"Shut up."

"This was the musical equivalent of boiled potatoes. Of soggy afternoons indoors. It was a world away from the excitement of garage and grime."

"Shut *up!*"

"This was the sound of New Labour: shining, polished but lacking any..."

Drunkenly, Peter picked up a weight and hurled it at the mirror. *Smash.* Cracks tore across its face.

"This was the middle-classes posing as..."

Seething, Peter hoisted up a kettlebell, spun it around and let it fly. *Crash.* Glass rained in a storm of twinkling shards.

Peter turned around and saw a television hanging from the wall. Something stirred inside his drunken soul. He picked up a barbell, ran forwards and drove it, like a lance, through the fragile screen.

Shit. Standing amid the broken glass, Peter reflected that that *might* have been a bad idea. Shamefacedly, with all of the rage spat out of him, he staggered from the gym hoping no cameras were watching. He crept up to his room and fell asleep across the middle of the bed.

Peter woke up two hours later with a raging headache. Memories *drip drip dripped* into his mind. *Shit.* Had anyone seen him?

Rolling out of bed and fumbling for one of the free bottles of water, Peter gagged on the sheer dryness of his mouth. Where was Tommy? *Where was Tommy?* If *he* had been this lairy, God knows what the guitarist would have done. Banged the Crown Prince's wife? Fought the Grand Mufti? Insulted Muhammad? He had to find him.

Staggering down the hall, Peter ran into Mahmud.

"Mr Baker?"

"Hello."

"I've been looking for you."

"Oh."

"You don't look well. Are you ill?"

"Yes."

"If you want to see a doctor, I ca---"

"Naw, you don't have to do anything. I, er, I, er – I'm just trying to find my friend."

Mahmud raised his chin and frowned.

"Mr Baker, have you been drinking?"

"No."

"Because you know that drinking alcohol is strictly illegal in the Kingdom of Saudi Arabia."

"Mahmud," said Peter, resting his hands on the man's shoulders and pushing him slightly back against the wall, "Mahmud, my friend. It's just medication. To help me sleep. Okay?"

"To help you sleep?"

Peter nodded, smiled and clapped Mahmud on the shoulder. The Saudi man stepped back under the force of the friendly blow. Peter staggered off down the corridor again, lurching around the corner and away from Mahmud's suspicious gaze. He thought that he had dealt with the situation as well as possible. It was just medication! What were these guys going to do? Give him a breathalyser?

Stumbling into Tommy's room, Peter looked around. It was empty. Through a haze of drunkenness, he was surprised to see that it was also tidy. The blankets were scrunched up, yes, but there was nothing on the floor, or the walls, or the surfaces. Peter scratched his face. He had expected broken glass, blood, full condoms and half-eaten food.

He was about to leave when he heard shouting outside. He saw, through the lacy curtains, that the door to the balcony was open. Peter pottered over, seeing that someone was outside. He drew back the curtain. Tommy was standing on the balcony, looking out across Riyadh.

Peter saw, in slow motion, that his hands were at his waist. Urine was arching out of his urethra and down through the air. Screams were erupting from the pavement as piss splattered on heads. In awe and horror, Peter walked around to look at Tommy's face. It bore an expression of pure serenity.

In the detention centre, Peter leaned against the wall. He wondered what his wife was going to say. What did it matter? Nagging would be music to his ears now that his back was against the unforgiving bricks of a Saudi cell. Besides, he was lucky. A poor migrant might have been dead rather than waiting for a plane ride home.

"Pete? Pete? Is that you?"

It was Tommy.

"Yeah, it's me. You okay?"

"Rock and roll, man," laughed the guitarist, "Rock and roll."

Anthropology

Oh…

Hey!

What are the chances?

It's Samantha, isn't it?

Yeah, we were at school together. Mrs Packman's class. You sat in front of me. You had blonde pigtails.

What are the chances?

So, what brings you here?

"Nasty Slut Taught A Lesson".

Christ, Samantha.

Did somebody write these lines or did you make them up yourself?

How did you get here?

Was it drugs? You tried weed. You tried cocaine. You tried crack. You ran out of money. It was this or prostitution.

Or maybe you like it. You want to make Daddy mad. Or you're an addict. You can't get enough of this.

Jesus, Samantha.

Have you had a kid? You look kind of older. Not just older. Old. You're trying to look young but it's obvious that you're not.

Good body, though.

Are you enjoying this? It looks kind of painful. It must be embarrassing that anyone can see it. But perhaps you're into that. Maybe it's your kink. I don't really understand it but that's your business I guess.

Look at you. What did you do after you finished here? Did they have a shower or did you travel home like this? All wet and stuff. Do you have a boyfriend? Do you tell him?

Does anyone want you?

Hey!

Darren isn't it?

What are the chances?

Yes, we were at school together. You had more hair then.

So, what brings you here?

You were searching for something innocent and I popped up?

Or you're into this.

You must be into this. I mean, it's not just porn. No, this is nasty stuff. Niche.

How long were been sitting there? One hour? Two? Three? And how often do you do this? Once a week? Twice a week? Every day?

You look funny.

Has anyone ever caught you?

Are you single? Do you have a girlfriend? Does she know what you're doing?

Why do you watch this? Do you have nothing better?

Does it feel good?

*What are your goals, Darren? How are you getting there?
No, I never dreamed of doing this but at least I'm getting
paid. At least I can save up and do something.*

I can.

I can.

*Do you think your mum would be prouder than mine if they
saw this? What did she teach you about women?*

*Are you going or are you going to watch another film? How
do know you've had enough? Do you ever have enough?*

*I remember falling over in school. You helped me up.
Imagined if we'd started talking. In another universe we
might be married now.*

Your Generation

"My phone isn't working."

Mariusz frowned at Maks.

"We're in the mountains, what do you expect?"

Maks dropped his phone into his lap and sighed. He looked out of the window at the dark, distant peaks, looking as impressed as if it had been an industrial estate. Mariusz looked at him with a cold, hard stare, as if wondering whose balls that sperm had actually emerged from.

Unscrewing the cap on his Coke, Mariusz raised the bottle to his lips. He knew that if he kept drinking he would have to take a piss before they got to Zakopane but a combination of boredom and annoyance compelled him to. He wondered why they had taken the coach and not the train. That damn saver's instinct.

He could hear the *thud thud thud-ing* of his son's music. What had he been thinking? He should have bought the kid a new smartphone and been done with it. But as Maks had turned 16 it had felt like a good time to connect him with his heritage. He had to be connected to *something* other than the fucking Internet.

Mariusz sat back and tried to ignore the gentle waves in his bladder, knowing that the more he thought about needing the toilet the more its seas would churn and boil.

At Zakopane, Mariusz shouldered his bag and Maks picked his up with a look of mild resentment. Mariusz bit his tongue. *How was it a burden to carry his own bag?* He shouldn't be surprised, he told himself. Maks often behaved as if it was a burden to carry his own body.

Their hotel was just off the high street – a nice, traditional place, Mariusz expected, but not so much that there was any risk of power outages or rats. He and Maks slogged through the thick, damp snow, which clung to their legs and the bottoms of their trousers. Maks winced as the cold sank into his flesh.

At the hotel, they trudged up to their room. Maks walked around, gazing at the surfaces.

"WiFi password?" Mariusz asked.

"Yup."

Mariusz swallowed his annoyance. It was natural for a boy to want to be in touch with his friends and family. Besides, Agnieszka had to know that they had got there. He trotted down to the reception again to find it.

That evening, the pair sat in the hotel restaurant. Mariusz drank a beer and Maks had a Coke. In the musky warmth of the log fire, the boy looked happier.

"Perhaps I'll buy you a cheeky beer before we leave," winked Mariusz.

"Nice."

Maks smiled, guardedly but genuinely.

"Just don't tell your mother."

"What are we doing tomorrow?"

"We're going to go and meet my cousin Igor. You'll like Igor."

"Why?"

Mariusz gazed deep into his son's blank expression.

"He's a good guy," he said, "And he can hold his drink."

"Oh."

Mariusz looked up at the mountains, rising grandly above them.

"I learned to ski round here," he smiled, "We spent every winter on the slopes. I wish you could have had that experience. It's a bad thing about being in England."

"Well, I've got bad balance anyway."

"So have I! Broke my leg, my hand..."

"Why did you do it then?"

Mariusz slumped into his beer. That night, he lay and heard Maks quietly snoring. He remembered sitting with him when he was days old, and then chided himself for being sentimental. At least the poor kid wasn't screaming now.

The hotel breakfast was everything that Mariusz had dreamed of and more. There was an enormous tray of fluffy, creamy scrambled eggs, sprawling ranks of sausages, at least five kinds of cheese, white bread, brown bread, pickled peppers, pickled mushrooms and great slabs of apple cake. Mariusz piled food onto his plate as if he did not expect to eat for the next year. Maks made himself a cheese and tomato sandwich.

"What do you call that?" Mariusz asked.

"Breakfast."

"You aren't hungry?"

"I'm never hungry in the morning."

"Yes," said Mariusz, dismayed, "But having a bit of everything at breakfast is the best thing about being in a hotel."

"Well," said Maks, thoughtfully, "Why can't they serve lunch like this? You know, a bit of everything?"

"Because..."

Mariusz thought about it.

"Because everyone is too full from breakfast."

He didn't believe it himself. He knew that lunches would now be a massive disappointment. The boy had *some* good ideas.

Mariusz and Maks pottered around Zakopane. It had been a long time since Mariusz had been there. His mum had died of heart disease 10 years before and his dad had moved in with his sister in Wrocław, where, bored and homesick, he had promptly died himself.

Mariusz still felt the touch of guilt when he thought about his father dying alone on his sister's bathroom floor. He would not have been there even if he had been in Poland, and he knew intellectually that cigarettes and processed meat had played more of a role than sad thoughts of his distant son, but he still regretted being on the other side of Europe.

The town was more touristy than Mariusz remembered. Garish plastic sledges rubbed shoulders with "Polska" hoodies and luminescent marijuana themed t-shirts. Mariusz realised, eyeing up the doughnuts through the window of Costa Coffee, that he was a tourist as well. He crossed the street and bought some mountain cheese.

"This is where the Nazis met the Soviets," he told Maks.

"This shop?"

"No, this *town*. They talked about what to do with our ancestors."

"*Our* ancestors?"

"Poles, stupid. They killed millions of them."

"Why?"

"Because they were evil, weren't they. They wanted to kill us all. But look who's still here!"

Maks gazed about the tourists and plastic sledges.

"Just be glad to be alive *now*," said Mariusz.

Later that morning, Mariusz and Maks took a bus to Poronin, where Mariusz had been raised. It was a little village to the north of Zakopane, embedded in the slopes, where houses and hotels with austere spiked roofs huddled in the snow. Mariusz had not visited in almost ten years, since Maks had been a boy. Here, at least, little had changed.

Mariusz remembered leaving the village in 2004. He had told his parents that he was coming back. He would save some money and return to build a house. He would have his own business – doing *something*. Had he believed it at the time?

Igor had inherited *his* father's house. Mariusz was disorientated to see it had been painted green. A German Shepherd was standing in a cage at one side of the house and barked in scandalised tones as he and Maks approached. Igor strode out in a t-shirt.

"Hello!" he cried in pantomimic English, "Hello my very good friends!"

He was balding and bearded, with a stomach that he could have perched a pint glass on.

"Mariusz!"

He shook Mariusz's hand with enough strength to choke an elephant.

"And this? My God. A man!"

He did the same to Maks, who winced.

"Come my very good friends!"

They followed Igor's giant waddling frame into the house and found themselves in a lumberjack's paradise. The walls were wooden. The floor was wooden. The stairs were wooden. Everything was wooden except for Igor's voice.

"Home!"

A stout young man was planted to the floor at the end of the hall, looking as if he had been whittled from a tree trunk. He looked bored and mildly suspicious but still shook their hands with enough of Igor's strength to hurt. Behind him was a smaller, skinnier young man. He had a fairly average build but looked downright emaciated compared to the rest of his family.

"My boys," said Igor in Polish, "Tomek and Piotr. Guess which one likes eating."

They walked into the dining room where a tall, thin woman with blonde hair and a frigid gaze was laying out plates of sour cucumber and potato salad. Mariusz wondered if spending hours cooking and cleaning so her husband could get drunk with a cousin he hardly ever saw was *really* how she wanted to spend her Saturday. Then again, Igor had doubtless had to go to his fair share of first communions and 75th birthday parties. That was marriage for you.

"This is my beautiful wife," said Igor.

"Of course," said Mariusz, "How are you Maria?"

"Good," she said, "My God, your boy has grown. They all do, don't they."

"Some of us never stop!" Igor announced sunnily, eating a handful of pretzels.

Mariusz introduced himself to Maria's mother, who was sitting in the corner looking as if she had just drunk a litre of lemon juice. She looked touched to be noticed and annoyed to be there.

"Drink!" Igor declared to no one in particular, opening a bottle of whisky.

"Not vodka?" Mariusz inquired.

"You know," said Igor, looking philosophical, "The older I get the more I want to try different things. We only live once after all."

He, Igor and Tomasz began to drink whisky and cokes as Maria served enough salad, soup, bread, cutlets, mashed potato, beetroot and cake to feed not just an army but an army travelling on foot across Eastern Europe. Mariusz found himself wondering, perhaps for the first time in his life, if he should have eaten *quite* so much for breakfast. Still, the booze kept flowing and lulled him into a state of half-drunk serenity.

"I couldn't live in England," said Igor seriously, "The English are an unhealthy people. When do Poles drink tea? When we are sick. When do the English drink tea? All the time."

He took another shot and looked around at Maks, who was picking at a piece of cake.

"Hey, kid," he barked.

"Hm?"

"You've barely said a word. Do you even speak Polish."

Maks nodded.

"Then say something."

"What do you want me to say?"

The Polish of the *Górale* who lived in the mountains was different from normal Polish anyway. With Maks's awkward, inexperienced pronunciation, it sounded especially comic to Igor's ears. He burst into a storm of laughter and even Maria grinned.

"Oh, don't worry, Maks," smiled Igor as the boy stared at him miserably, "I'm just messing with you. Imagine how funny I would seem in England."

He grimaced slightly as he saw he had embarrassed Maks.

"Tomasz, Piotr, why don't you take your cousin Maks to see the dogs or something? You don't want to sit with us old men all day."

They left the room and he breathed a sigh of relief.

"Young people can be so sensitive," he mused, opening another bottle, "I called Tomek a fucking idiot the other day and he punched a hole through the wall."

Mariusz nodded understandingly.

"Did you talk to Tomek?" Mariusz burped as the bus slipped and slided back to Zakopane.

"No, I talked to Piotr."

"Oh? What did he say?"

"He said he likes hacking into people's Instagram accounts."

"Oh."

The next morning, after a slightly less titanic breakfast, Mariusz had planned a hike up the mountains. He wanted to show his son the snowy peaks where he had spent his childhood. The cold gnawed the legs as they slogged up the slopes. Maks maintained a disposition of silent gloom.

The pair walked into a clearing, where, between the trees, they could see the great white mountains and the town lying beneath them. Mariusz watched Maks look down and then turn away.

"That's the problem with your generation," he said, disdainfully, "You're so hooked to Facebook, and Instagram, and Snapchat, you can't appreciate a beautiful view like this."

"Do you have to be so negative," said Maks, stabbing his ski pole into the snow.

"*I'm* negative?"

"Everything is always about "my generation". "My generation" has it easy. "My generation" doesn't understand real life."

"I dunno," said Mariusz, bewildered, "*Do* you? I'm just trying to help you appreciate things."

"By making me feel bad," Maks said, "Very inspirational."

He walked further up the path and then turned around.

"Anyway, no one uses Facebook."

They walked on in silence. Maks's face was at its most inscrutable. Mariusz thought about what he had said. He had to admit that he had not been wholly honest with his son. When he had said he wanted Maks to appreciate "things" he had not meant *life* as much as he had meant *him*. He remembered years of getting home from the construction site, eating lunch and heading out to freelance decorating jobs. Now, Maks acted like their home and everything inside it had always been there. But he saw the kid's point. He didn't want to make him feel like a charity case.

"Dad?"

"Yeah?"

"Where are we *going*?"

"Well," sighed Mariusz, "We're going to..."

He looked around. The forest was thicker than he remembered it being. There was a rocky outcrop he had never seen before.

Had they missed their turning?

"We're going left," he said, "It's a shortcut."

The path, if it *was* a path, took them slightly down the hill towards a stream. The ground beneath their feet was muddy and slick. They had to push their way through needle-bristling branches. Mariusz held them carefully to stop them whipping into Maks.

"Is this *really* the way?"

"I *told* you," said Mariusz, with agitation creeping into his tone, "It's a shortcut. We have to walk beside the stream."

It had to go *somewhere*. Mariusz wiped his face and looked down the stream and the loose rocks beside it. Could Maks walk there safely?

As soon as the thought arrived, Mariusz felt his legs disappear. Time inched forwards with dismaying inevitability. He fell like a bag of bricks, landing on his ass, with his foot twisted beside him. Pain shot up his leg, as if a knife was being dragged from his ankle to his thigh.

"*Fuck!*"

He tried to stand but his foot was as much use as a cracked fishbowl. Maks looked shellshocked.

"I'm okay!" Mariusz wheezed, "I'm okay!"

He tried to walk. Every time he put his left foot down he felt like screaming. It was as if a enormous man was rocking backwards and forwards on a chair and every time its leg was being driven into his foot.

"Dad, are you okay?"

"Fine."

He sat down and took off his shoe – an experience like skinning a deer and *being* the deer simultaneously. His foot resembled a steak, cooked medium-rare.

"Jesus, Dad."

Mariusz picked up a handful of snow and pressed it against the skin.

"Alright," he said, "I'm not going to lie to you. I'm *not* okay. It hurts like hell. But I'm okay to keep walking."

"Are you sure?"

"Well, we have to get down this bloody mountain don't we."

"We could call for help."

"And have you sitting here in the cold while they look for us? No. We're getting down this mountain."

138

So, they stumbled on. The pain dulled. It did not *improve* but Mariusz felt more like he was being struck by a hammer than stabbed with a knife. He took this to mean that he had sprained his ankle and not broken it.

Mariusz found himself sinking into silent prayer. He was guiltily areligious, and had spent no more time in churches since 2004 than he had spent in laundrettes, but some things compelled religiosity and children were prime among them.

Maks, beside him, methodically stepped from rock to rock. He had an almost mathematical approach to walking. Mariusz had often fumed about his cold, unfathomable demeanour but now he found himself admiring it. There was not a hint of panic or self-pity.

The stream snaked down the mountain. Gasping on the dense cold air, Mariusz prayed that it travelled somewhere civilised.

"Doing okay, mate?"

"Sure," said Maks.

"You're a natural."

There was silence. Water gurgled and branches snapped.

"Thanks."

Mariusz could feel water seeping into his boots. He was glad to feel its frigid coldness on his injured foot but he knew that it would travel upwards through his body. Thank God he had bought Maks a brand new pair.

Looking up on the slope on the opposite side of the stream, Mariusz noticed something. On the top the trees seemed to disappear. It was not a matter of perspective. The forest broke.

"It's a path."

"Really?"

"Really."

"Not a shortcut?"

"Not a shortcut."

Edging across the stream, they picked their way up the slope. Mariusz drove his walking stick into the mud with all his strength and used the thing to pull himself up the hillside. With his other hand, he clung onto branches and rocks. As he reached the top of the slope, Maks took his arm and helped to drag him onto flat ground. Mariusz resisted the instinct to complain.

It *was* a path. It unravelled, slowly, gently, towards the bottom of the mountain. Mariusz saw the stream disappearing leftwards, into thicker reaches of the forest. He practically danced down the slush-slick slope.

"You should go to the hospital," said Maks, as they sat in a restaurant, in front of the fire, enjoying the outer reaches of tolerable heat.

"Nah," said Mariusz, wishing he need never reach the bottom of his bowl of stew or glass of beer, "They'll tell me to rest it. So, why bother walking there?"

He lifted a final spoonful of pork, cabbage and tomato into his mouth and thought with deep seriousness about ordering another plate.

"Perha---"

He put his hand to his hip. Instead of his smooth, hard wallet he found his leg. What? He tried the other one. Empty as well. *Shit.*

"I think I dropped my wallet on the mountain," he said.

His cards had been in there. How was he going to pay for the meal? How was he going to pay for the *hotel*?

"No problem," said Maks, taking out his card, "I'll get this."

"*You'll* get this?"

"Sure, I have money."

"How?"

"The Internet," shrugged Maks, "I build websites."

Mariusz looked at his son, lost even for sounds.

"You never told me about this."

"You never asked."

General Chat

Gool | 12.11.21 | 21.26

@gummo, tell @ratshit to stop posting pr0n.

Gool | 12.11.21 | 21.28

Actually, ban him.

Ratshit | 12.11.21 | 21.30

fuck u snitch

Ratshit | 12.11.21 | 21.30

wasnt even porn she was just nekkid

Gool | 12.11.21 | 21.34

I don't come here to see naked sluts.

Ratshit | 12.11.21 | 21.40

wtf you come here 4

Gool | 12.11.21 | 21.40

To teach and to learn.

Ratshit | 12.11.21 | 21.42

lol

Problematrix | 12.11.21 | 21.43

This guy should be gassed.

Problematrix | 12.11.21 | 21.43

I'm not being ironic by the way.

King Boon | 12.11.21 | 22.04

Is this Frenchie?

"Man Arrested For "Terroristic Threats" Claims He Was Trying To Stop Satan"

Ratshit | 12.11.21 | 22.10

who tf is Frenchie

Gool | 12.11.21 | 22.13

Kids on this forum don't even know who Frenchie is. No culture.

Ratshit | 12.11.21 | 22.15

eat my ass ninja

Pisstopher Bitchens | 12.11.21 | 22.15

Frenchie made the forum *this* forum came from.

Ratshit | 12.11.21 | 22.18

eh

Pisstopher Bitchens | 12.11.21 | 22.24

SmokeBreak

Ratshit | 12.11.21 | 22.28

u ninjas old as fukk

Token Jap | 12.11.21 | 22.31

It's him. He facedoxxed years ago on SB. Look.

Gool | 12.11.21 | 22.33

Damn, the last ten years did a number on this guy.

King Boon | 12.11.21 | 22.34

WTF is this!?

"Mr Simpson (45) threatened to bomb the offices of hosting companies across the US and Europe if they did not remove certain websites"

Ratshit | 12.11.21 | 22.37

consequences of meth

Pisstopher Bitchens | 12.11.21 | 22.39

Must be about The Curse.

Ratshit | 12.11.21 | 22.41

my man said "curse"

Gool | 12.11.21 | 22.42

Don't talk about that nonsense.

Pisstopher Bitchens | 12.11.21 | 22.44

It isn't nonsense. Every – I mean *every* – well-known poster from that forum went mad.

Ratshit | 12.11.21 | 22.46

bro u got 2 b mad 2 be a "well-known poster"

Pisstopher Bitchens | 12.11.21 | 22.47

KenDoll – Killed his wife.

BenG – Got arrested for doing coke in Singapore.

JuliusSleazer – The jam jar thing[*].

PureRussian – Also killed his wife.

Doom – Was an actual terrorist.

Source: "SmokeBreak: The Honour Roll!"

Ratshit | 12.11.21 | 22.50

again you dont hear about posters real lives in general because we have shit jobs wank and sleep

Pisstopher Bitchens | 12.11.21 | 22.53

You weren't on the fucking forums. You don't know what it was like.

Ratshit | 12.11.21 | 22.56

dis ninja talk like he was in vietnam

King Boon | 12.11.21 | 23.01

He has a point. SB got dark, for sure, but that's how forums are. A bunch of freaks get thrown together and piss each other off.

Gool | 12.11.21 | 23.03

That is basically my argument against immigration.

Pisstopher Bitchens | 12.11.21 | 23.04

It was more than that bruh. It wasn't just an individual thing. It was this fukking butterfly effect. You could have a thread about a vidya gaem and two hundred pages later people would be talking about four teenagers attempting ritual suicide. That was what Frenchie meant by The Curse. He thought there was some kind of force in the site itself.

Gool | 12.11.21 | 23.06

He thought he could write poems and that he could teach himself to suck his own dick.

Gummo | 12.11.21 | 23.07

Talk about something else guys. Didn't we start this forum to get away from that shithole?

Token Jap | 12.11.21 | 23.09

You know, R_V thought the site was some kind of military experiment – MKULTRA but for the Internet.

Problematrix | 12.11.21 | 23.12

R_V was a Jewish cunt who jumped out of a window.

Token Jap | 12.11.21 | 23.13

Yer but look how Frenchie "lost control" of the site. That never made sense. We just went along with it because nobody liked him.

Gool | 12.11.21 | 23.20

Skullf**k said he bought it off Frenchie. I never knew much about him but he was a better mod.

Pisstopher Bitchens | 12.11.21 | 23.22

What sort of experiment did R_V say it was?

Token Jap | 12.11.21 | 23.26

Sort of facilitating interactions and events to test and guide people's behaviour in online spaces. Working out how to control the Internet.

Ratshit | 12.11.21 | 22.28

control deez nuts boi

Ratshit | 12.11.21 | 22.28

i just woke up i cant read all this shit talk about something else or im going back to bed

Gummo | 12.11.21 | 23.33

The idea was to predict responses based on input.

Gummo | 12.11.21 | 23.34

147

If you could predict responses accurately enough you could also produce them.

Problematrix | 12.11 | 23.35

So, you could manipulate online discourse with little input.

Token Jap | 12.11.21 | 23.36

Wut?

Gummo | 12.11.21 | 23.37

The problem is that there is too much possible input and there are too many potential responses.

Problematrix | 12.11.21 | 23.38

It was possible to develop heuristics to develop but it was impossible to systematise them entirely.

Pisstopher Bitchens | 12.11.21 | 23.40

Who the fuck is talking here?

Token Jap | 12.11.21 | 23.41

This some kind of troll?

Ratshit | 12.11.21 | 22.44

Some things turned out to be impossible to anticipate because of the interaction of different stimuli that had yet to be integrated into the models.

Ratshit | 12.11.21 | 22.46

But the results were still interesting and can still contribute to the production of more sophisticated modelling.

Ratshit | 12.11.21 | 22.47

Especially with the greater processing ability of artificial intelligence.

Token Jap | 12.11.21 | 23.49

Is anyone here normal please?

Pisstopher Bitchens | 12.11.21 | 23.51

I don't think anyone here was ever normal.

Gool | 12.11.21 | 23.52

WTF is going on!?

Gummo | 12.11.21 | 23.53

The experiment has ended. Thank you for participating.

Token Jap | 12.11.21 | 23.53

What the hell?

Pisstopher Bitchens | 12.11.21 | 23.54

Boon texted me. He says he can't log on.

Gool | 12.11.21 | 23.55

Is this a joke guys?

Gool | 12.11.21 | 23.57

Is this a prank?

Gool | 12.11.21 | 23.59

Come on guys

Gool | 12.11.21 | 23.59

please

Printed in Great Britain
by Amazon